D0496007

Flesh and Bones

BAINTE DEN STOC

WITHDRAWN FROM
DÚN LAOGHAIRE-RATHDOWN COUNTY
LIBRARY STOCK

www.rbooks.co.uk

Also by Alan Durant and available in Definitions:

Blood

Flesh and Bones

ALAN DURANT

BAINTE DEN STOC

WITHDRAWN FROM
DÚN LAOGHAIRE-RATHDOWN COUNTY
LIBRARY STOCK

DEFINITIONS
in association with The Bodley Head

FLESH AND BONES
A DEFINITIONS BOOK 978 0 099 456551

First published in Great Britain by Definitions,
an imprint of Random House Children's Books
A Random House Group Company

This edition published 2008

3 5 7 9 10 8 6 4 2

Copyright © Alan Durant, 2008

The right of Alan Durant to be identified as the author of this work
has been asserted in accordance with the Copyright, Designs and Patents Act 1988.

All rights reserved. No part of this publication may be reproduced,
stored in a retrieval system, or transmitted in any form or by
any means, electronic, mechanical, photocopying, recording
or otherwise, without the prior permission of the publishers.

The Random House Group Limited supports the Forest Stewardship Council (FSC),
the leading international forest certification organization. All our titles that are printed on Greenpeace-approved FSC certified paper carry the FSC logo. Our paper procurement policy can be found at
www.rbooks.co.uk/environment

Set in Sabon

Definitions are published by Random House Children's Books,
61–63 Uxbridge Road, London W5 5SA

www.**kidsatrandomhouse**.co.uk
www.**rbooks**.co.uk

Addresses for companies within The Random House Group Limited
can be found at: www.randomhouse.co.uk/offices.htm

THE RANDOM HOUSE GROUP Limited Reg. No. 954009

A CIP catalogue record for this book is available from the British Library.

Printed and bound in Great Britain by
CPI Bookmarque, Croydon, CR0 4TD

Acknowledgement

This book took a long time to write (too long, some would say) but it would never have been completed at all if not for the invaluable assistance of a few people, whom I should like to thank here: my editor, Charlie Sheppard, for her faith, patience and amazing understanding; Kate, for her profound friendship and encouragement (and connections!); her uncle, Father Matthew, and the other monks of Ampleforth, whose hospitality and openness during my brief stay with them provided a key spark of inspiration; my oldest daughter, Amy, for her unflinching critical eye; and last, but by no means least, my wife, Jinny, for her constant love and support through thick and thin. I dedicate this book to each and every one of them with immense gratitude, warmth and appreciation.

Alan Durant

The Times, 13 June 1999

MEDIEVAL MYSTERY OF SKULL AND 'SCRATCHCARD'

A yellowing piece of parchment found beneath the altar of a ruined monastic church could be the world's earliest known scratchcard, archaeological experts believe.

The 10in by 8in document, whose authenticity is currently being researched with the help of the British Library, is considered to date from the late fifteenth century. It was discovered during excavations at Maundle Abbey near York.

The parchment, known as an incunabula, features three illuminated characters side by side, with a text promising the winner a spiritual reward. It is thought to be an indulgence sold by the Church to guilty Christians seeking forgiveness for their sins. Dr Malcolm Wagstaff, who is heading the excavation, says that the parchment may well be worth hundreds of thousands of pounds.

The dig also uncovered a skull, which it is believed may be the last remains of the monastery's founder, St Geronimus. If confirmed, this would be a very significant find for the Church. Dr Wagstaff said that while it was too soon to make any such claims, initial tests and research revealed that the skull dated back several centuries.

Dr Wagstaff told reporters that there was no evidence that the incunabula and the skull were connected, although, he added, this could not be ruled out. Tests continue.

Part One

Chapter 1

The skull made me feel sad, deeply sad. Staring into those cavities where eyes had once been, imagining the flesh that once covered the bare white bone . . . it brought a lump to my throat. Quite apart from anything else, a skull was a death's head, and death made me think of Mum; this skull more than any other, 'cause it had been dug up from its five-hundred-year-old rest a year to the day after Mum died. A whole year had gone by and I was still a mess. But then how could you ever get over something as terrible as that? Could there *be* anything as terrible as that? It seemed to me that even if I was five hundred years old like that skull, I could never come to terms with Mum's death.

I picked up the sheet of paper on which Dad had noted the main findings from the physical anthropologist's report. It was headed 'Brother Boniface'. How they must have laughed when someone had come up with that name. I could see why it had seemed appropriate: Boniface was a saint's name, and what was a skull but a bony face? But I hated it. It wasn't his name, was it? Nobody knew what his name had been. The one thing they knew for certain was that he wasn't St Geronimus the Venerable. Dr Wagstaff's enthusiasm for this theory had been misplaced – so Dad said. He didn't have much time for Dr Wagstaff. The two of them had worked together before on another dig and they hadn't exactly hit it off. Dad dismissed Wagstaff as a 'sensationalist', always trying to bend the facts to fit his theories.

So who was the person whose skull I was now staring into? A novice monk apparently. According to the report, he'd been in his mid-teens when he'd died: 'Boniface was a male Caucasian of European ancestry and stood about 5' 4" tall.' The same height as me, which would have made him below average now, though in those days I reckoned it would probably have been quite tall. No one would have called him 'short arse' the way some of the kids at school did me. Not that I cared any more. What were a few taunts next to what I'd been through?

I stared once more into the hollow sightless eyes and again had that overwhelming feeling of sadness. I'd lost my mother, and so had he, I thought – well, actually, no, she'd abandoned him. We'd done a project on monastic life in RS and I knew that in medieval times parents put their into monasteries the way some parents these days pa their offspring off to boarding school. Only going into monastery was for life; there was no going home for the holidays. It was final – final as death. How could any mother do that?

My eyes moved to the bigger cavity in the crown of the skull where the fatal blow had been struck before the head had been severed from the body. As yet, no one knew why. Had the boy suffered? Had he had time to know what was happening, to register the identity of his killer – or had death been instantaneous? Dad said that the experts inclined towards the latter theory. They'd finished all their tests, carbon dating and all the rest – they knew when he lived, how tall he'd been, how he'd died; now they'd passed the skull on to Dad to try to discover what he'd really looked like. That was Dad's job: putting flesh on the bones – well, clay anyway.

Once again I gazed into the eyes. The eyes! I started, blinked, frowned. The skull was eyeless. *But brown eyes had gazed back*. It wasn't possible, but it shook me all the same – not just the eyes, but for a second I'd heard a sound too, oddly muffled like someone talking to you when your head was under water. I turned to see if anyone had come into the room. I was alone.

* * *

…t evening me and Dad and Dad's brother, Uncle Jack, …ting having supper. Jack on his favourite subject: *what …'d do if I won the lottery*. Tonight he was going to buy himself a yacht – 'A great gin palace,' he said – and cruise around the world, visiting exotic places.

'You've as much chance of that happening as Wagstaff has of making a sensible diagnosis,' said Dad.

Jack raised his hands in a stop-right-there gesture; pursed his lips. 'You may scoff,' he said. 'But I have faith. One day it's going to happen, you'll see. And then you'll laugh on the other side of your face.'

'Not me.' Dad again. 'I'd wish you luck, Jack, because that's when you'd need it. You may need incredibly good fortune to win the thing; but not to let it ruin your life when you do – now that's when you'd need all the luck in the world. Riches – and especially unearned riches – never brought anyone happiness. Winning the lottery has ruined more lives than it's benefited, I'm certain of that.'

'Ah, you scientists,' Jack tutted. 'You have no imagination – no soul.' He turned to me. 'Isn't that right, Liam?'

I shrugged. 'I reckon there are better things to put your faith in than the lottery.'

'Oh yes, and what might they be?'

'Well' – a hesitation – 'God.'

'God? Now you *are* clutching at straws. Tell him, Will.'

Dad sighed. 'I can't say I find either helpful.'

'I suppose you believe in science,' Jack irked.

'It seems as good a thing as any to put your faith in. At least it doesn't promise what it can't deliver.' Dad pushed at a dollop of mash with his fork. 'Take that skull I'm working on. What good did believing in God do him, poor beggar?'

I wasn't having that. 'You don't know that. Maybe he was better off dying. Maybe he went to heaven and he's looking down on us right now, shaking his head at what a mess we've made of things putting all our faith in science or the lottery.'

'Hey, don't knock the lottery,' Jack sparked. 'Anyway, didn't I hear they found some kind of scratchcard in with that monk of yours?'

'It was an incunabula, offering absolution from sins,' said Dad. 'And I think the reward it offered was to be collected *after* death.'

'After death?' Jack was aghast. 'What's the use in that?'

'If you believed in hell and damnation, which most people did in those days, then getting rid of your sins was essential: you didn't want to live for ever in the burning fires of hell. So you did everything you could to be absolved from your sins – go on a pilgrimage, buy an indulgence, give money to a church or monastery – so that when you died, you'd be rewarded with a place in heaven. And knowing this, the Church cashed in any way they could. Selling incunabula, or spiritual scratchcards, was just one wheeze they came up with.'

My hackles were up and I couldn't let it pass. 'You think science has got so much to be proud of? What's it ever done for us except help create nuclear missiles and mutant tomatoes?'

Dad smiled wearily. 'That's ridiculously simplistic, Liam, and you know it. I'm going back to work.'

In bed that night I picked at the conversation – science, the lottery, the skull, God . . . I hadn't always believed in God. It was only since Mum died that I'd gone down that route – and it had brought me some comfort where nothing else had been able to. I'd talked to friends, doctors, bereavement counsellors, listened to countless words of advice, sympathy and consolation, but nothing could break through the crust of despair that had grown over me. Certainly not Dad. Not that he'd really tried.

I'd gone into a church to annoy Dad as much as anything. I couldn't bear the way he seemed so matter-of-fact about our tragedy. He just carried on working with his old bones as if nothing had changed. When I told him that one of the counsellors had suggested talking to a priest, Dad had dismissed it out of hand. 'Pie in the sky,' he'd called it. 'A waste of time.' So I, who hadn't been thinking of following up the suggestion, did so the very next day.

The priest, Father Christopher, was very approachable. He invited me to a service. And I liked it. I liked being part of a . . . well, yes, a family. It made me feel wanted, supported. I found praying a release. I could say what I felt without having anyone opposite, pitying or judging or analysing. There was comfort too in the idea of an afterlife – that monk in heaven looking down . . .

The bones are false.

The words came out of the air. Or were they in my head? Had they insinuated themselves in one of those nano-seconds of unconsciousness when my eyes had closed and almost at once opened again. I sat up, knew myself to be wide awake, my room just as it always was, the sky outside dark, starless, a fuzzy glimmer at the window from the streetlights.

Foul deeds. Murder. The Black Art.

The same voice again, and this time a figure too, superimposed on my vision like one of those overhead projector overlays they were so fond of at school: a boy, about my own age, earnest brown eyes staring out from under the cowl of a black serge habit. A monk's habit.

Brother Boniface.

CHAPTER 2

The visions and the voices became more and more frequent. I heard whispers of bones and murder, saw shadowy hooded figures – and the eyes, always the eyes, staring out at me, imploring me in. I was drawn to the skull compulsively. It no longer made me feel sad. Now it evoked in me a range of new feelings – fascination, elation, terror.

I watched Dad in his workshop with his ultrasound equipment, attempting to gauge the depth of the tissue there would have been on the living face of the skull. As Dad had explained a number of times, the results were only approximate – they gave you 'average' information and you couldn't be sure your subject had been average. Some people had small heads, some – Neanderthals, for example – had large ones. But you got some basic guidelines – 'Good enough for someone like Wagstaff, but not for a proper scientist.' Dad preferred the anatomical method. This is where his real expertise came to the fore. He drew on his deep knowledge of the muscles, glands and fat pads that most affect the way people look to give life to the skull.

It wasn't the first time I had watched Dad carry out this operation, but I'd never before been affected like this. I could barely watch as he painstakingly sculpted the defining anatomical structures onto the skull. I winced as if these structures were being applied to my own head: the zygomaticus muscle between the eyes, the parotid gland above the left eye, the orbicularis oris at the bridge of the nose . . . There were seven structures in all, and with each one, my hand went involuntarily to the corresponding area on my own face. I felt giddy, like I'd been given an anaesthetic and was in that mid state between consciousness and unconsciousness when light intensifies and sound muffles.

Brother Martin will be your keeper. He will make sure that you are well looked after and that you carry out the vows and duties you are bounden to.

Two figures in tunics whispering in the darkness.

You know too much, and knowledge is a dangerous, dangerous thing.

Murder. The Black Art.

'Are you all right, Liam?' A voice floating in the ether. Then Dad's face coming into focus.

I blinked, squinted. 'I feel sort of faint.' My breathing was fast, desperate, as if I were drowning.

'Slow down. Deep breaths.' Dad's voice again. And yet, no, not Dad's.

And then another voice. *The indulgences are worthless. The bones are false. There is no truth in them.*

A cloister. A hooded figure. The sound of bells.

And then nothing.

'Thomas, Thomas.' He opened his eyes and his mother was sitting at the end of the bed. Her hair was down, flowing about her pale face in all its golden glory. He loved that. He loved her eyes too, gazing at him, smiling sadly – sapphire blue with a fleck of brown to one side of the dark pupils. He blinked in the dusty sunlight, his eyes and mind coming slowly into focus. He took in the burned tallow candle at his bedside, remembered what day it was.

'Mother,' he said simply. But his thoughts were far from simple. How could he bear to leave her? How could she bear to part from him?

'You must bathe and dress, Thomas,' she said. 'I'll have Robin fill the tub.' She paused. 'The Lord knows when you will next have such an opportunity.' As she spoke these words, tears glistened in her eyes.

His pity for her overcame his own apprehension. 'Why, Mother, don't be sad,' he said gaily. 'That's one of the benefits of becoming a monk.'

It was well known that monks did not believe in regular bathing, once a month or so being considered quite sufficient; to bathe more frequently was unholy self-indulgence. His own family bathed at least twice a week. His mother insisted upon it. Now all that was going to change. Everything was going to change. His old life was over. Today he was being taken into Maundle Abbey to begin his training as a novice monk.

When his mother left to supervise Robin, he lay back on his bolster and looked up at the curved roof-beams. He wondered for a moment what his new bedroom would be like. The monks slept in dormitories, he knew that. There would be none of the privacy he had been accustomed to at home these past months, since his older brother Giles had gone to live with a wealthy churchman to learn to be a gentleman. With Giles there had been no chance of privacy at all. He had a way of discovering any hiding place. He would lift every floorboard if he felt there was something to uncover, no matter how trivial it might be. He took after their father in that way. As the owner of a lucrative goldsmith's shop, Father was always wary of theft, and was meticulous about security. He watched over his wares like a hawk. His craftsmen even wore special sheepskin aprons to catch the tiny gold chippings from their labour, so that nothing of any value was wasted. As the oldest son, Giles would take over their father's business one day, and Thomas knew he would be suited to the task in a way that he himself would never have been. He was much more like his mother – trusting, haphazard, devout. His business would be to serve God, and he was prepared to do so, though he could not help but feel apprehension at taking this new step and leaving behind all he knew and loved.

Thomas examined his chamber for the last time. His eyes took in the wall-hangings, peacock blue with a pattern of yellow roses, the badge of his father's family, and the dark oak chest, chipped and scarred with age, decorated with carvings of mythical beasts. His gaze settled on the objects on top of the chest: the off-white skulls of a fox and a ferret, complete with teeth, which had been his greatest treasures through his boyhood. His mother hated them. 'Horrible old bones', she called them, and he smiled now as he recalled it. They would give him nightmares, she said, and she couldn't understand what he saw in them. Her incomprehension only deepened when he told her that he found the skulls strangely comforting – not in the way that so many people these days found succour in sacred bones and relics (there was nothing sacred about the animal skulls), but because they had a lifelike quality about them, even in death, that was reassuring. He didn't find the fierce set of their teeth frightening. His imagination put flesh upon the bones and they became his friends. He hated the thought of leaving them now. He had little faith that they would be properly looked after.

The bones are false, the indulgences worthless. There is no truth in them. It is nothing but wicked deceit and greed.

They practise the Black Art.

'Thomas, come!' Mum's voice calling.

But, no, how could it be? Mum was dead. Dead and buried.

I heard from the street the grating whine of the failing fan-belt like the shriek of an injured animal. I heard the wild crescendo of the accelerating engine, the squeal of tyres skidding, the thump and smash of metal and glass imploding as they crashed into thick, unyielding concrete. Then a terrible, ear-exploding scream.

I woke up; realized it was my own.

CHAPTER 3

Dad took me to the doctor, told him how I'd seemed to lose consciousness. For several minutes he'd been unable to communicate with me, he said; then suddenly I'd come to with a piercing scream ('a scream loud enough to wake the dead' is how Uncle Jack had described it – with no trace of irony. If only, I'd thought. If only . . .). The doctor couldn't find anything wrong. He talked of prescribing some kind of sedative but Dad would have none of it. I knew that Mum had taken Prozac and other stuff – and that Dad hadn't agreed with it. He didn't want his son to have anything to do with drugs and he told the doctor so.

'He's suffering from grief, that's all,' he said. 'He'll get over it in time, in his own way.'

He told the doctor what had happened: that Mum had died in a car crash, that her car had gone out of control and smashed into a concrete wall. The way he told it was so cool and matter-of-fact it was like he was telling the doctor the plot of a movie he'd seen. There wasn't a tremor of emotion in his voice. I wondered sometimes whether he felt any sense of loss at all. As soon as the doctor left, he went back to work, and I lay in bed seething.

Uncle Jack came by later.

'How are you feeling?' he asked.

'OK.' I shrugged. 'Tired.' Tired of carrying this grief around like an Olympic torch.

'We were worried about you.'

'Sorry. I didn't mean to cause all this fuss. I know how busy Dad is.'

'Yeah. That skull. He's obsessed with it.'

I thought about that. *Was* he obsessed with it? I was. 'There's something strange about that skull,' I said at last.

'How, strange?' Uncle Jack raised an eyebrow mock-quizzically.

'I don't know. When I'm near it, staring at it, it seems to take a hold of me.' I paused. 'I hear things.'

'Hear things!' Uncle Jack's voice teetered on laughter. 'What things?'

I sighed. I wished I hadn't said anything, but it was too late now. 'Voices, whispering. And I see things too.'

'Now you *are* starting to worry me.'

'It sounds mad, I know,' I conceded. 'It's all so confused. I saw Mum crashing her car. But before that I saw this boy, about my age, a young monk. He was in bed. His mother woke him. He was about to enter a monastery.' It came in sections, as if I was recalling a dream. 'But it's like I *was* him, like I was living his life – or he was living it through me. I see his thoughts, his dreams even.' I sighed again. I was starting to scare myself.

But for the first time Uncle Jack actually looked interested. He put down his newspaper – opened at the racing selections, of course. 'Maybe you've got some sort of gift,' he suggested quite seriously. 'You know, second sight. It could be very significant.'

I laughed. 'I can't tell you this week's winning lottery numbers or who's going to win the Grand National, Uncle Jack, if that's what you're thinking.'

Uncle Jack raised a hand. 'You can scoff,' he said, 'but there *are* people who have these paranormal abilities.'

Jack's seriousness had the opposite effect on me. It made me smile and shy away from the possibilities he was suggesting. 'Not me. I'm just your idiot nephew with an over-active imagination.' But still, I thought when I was alone again, it was strange the effect that skull had on me.

* * *

The next day I felt stronger, more normal. I got up and had breakfast, then went to Dad's workshop. There were photographs and sketches of the skull from many different viewpoints pinned up on a large board, in front of which Dad was now standing, contemplating his subject. The work had moved on to the next stage now – the clay sculpting. The skull rested on its plinth, still eyeless, but now fleshed with clay. I watched silently for a few moments, before giving a quiet cough. Dad turned and looked at me, but for some instants seemed unable to recognize his son. 'Oh, hello, Liam,' he uttered eventually.

I nodded at the skull. 'I see you're making progress.'

'Yes. Just having a few difficulties with the ears.' He sighed. 'The problem is the bones don't give you much of an indication like they do with the other features. I know where the centre of the ears should be located' – he pointed with his pencil – 'and that their angle would usually be in line with the angle of the jaw, but whether they were large or small or how the lobes hung, well, it's just about impossible to say.'

I had to smile at Dad's discomfort. How he hated imprecision or uncertainty. He had to know or at least explain everything absolutely.

A picture flashed in my mind. 'He had quite small ears,' I said without thinking. 'A bit like mine.'

Dad frowned. 'How on earth could you know that?'

'Just a feeling. Intuition.'

Dad huffed. 'Speculation more like. I have enough of that from that damn fool Wagstaff. Now he's on about dark practices. His latest theory is that the boy was a victim of a ritualistic pagan sacrifice, which culminated in beheading.'

I have to admit I was intrigued. 'Well, he could be right, couldn't he?'

'He could be, but he could equally well not be. That's my point. It's just speculation. Why not wait till we've got more evidence and then make an informed judgement. He just wants publicity.' Dad turned back to his subject and considered it carefully. 'You could be right about the ears, though,' he said at last. 'It would fit.' He put his hands to the side of the skull as if measuring.

'Thanks,' I said. 'Oh, and by the way, I'm feeling much better, in case you're interested . . .' I might as well have saved my breath 'cause Dad was back at work and deaf to anything but the sound of his own musings.

I sat on a stool at the back of the room and watched him working. Had he always been like this – obsessed by his job, unemotional, uninterested in anything else? So lacking in feeling that he could dismiss his wife's tragic, violent death with barely a glimmer of misery? I'd only ever seen him cry once, and then it was like a shutter had come down: he'd just withdrawn even further into his work, carried on with his sculpting and moulding. Even when Mum was alive, it had been me who'd tried to comfort her on those awful nights when I found her sobbing wretchedly in her room. I hadn't really known what to do. I'd just put my arms around her, whispered, 'It's all right, Mum,' desperately hoping it would be.

Suddenly she was there, her golden hair worn up beneath a simple black linen cap. She stepped forward and embraced him and he smelled the scent of violets.

'Be good, Thomas. The Lord be with you.' Her voice was quiet, hoarse with breaking emotion. She clung onto him as if she could not let him go, even though she knew she must. He clung to her too. How could he possibly let her go? How could he live without her?

'Madam, we must leave. I have business to attend to.' His father's voice, uncomfortable, peremptory. If he could have avoided coming, he would have. He hated leaving his shop during business hours. Who could say what disaster might not befall it while he was away?

'You leave him in the best of hands, madam, sir.' Abbot Eidric gave a small nod to each and smiled reassuringly, in his hands a beautifully crafted gold plate encrusted with rubies, the goldsmith's gift to the abbey on taking his son into service. The abbot's eyes lighted on Thomas and were so full of grace and kindness that the new novice felt suddenly soothed and comforted. The abbot gestured to a tall monk at his side. 'Brother Martin is the master of the novices . . .'

His heart has gone.

Foul deeds. Murder. Necromancy.

My temples throbbed. I closed my eyes, opened them. The skull stared back at me with its deep, hollow eyes. Imploring.

Chapter 4

Foul deeds. Murder. Necromancy. The words nagged at me like flies on a hot summer's day. What was going on? Where were these words coming from? And the visions? Were they just dreams? One moment I was in my own reality and then suddenly I'd slipped back in time to another. My English teachers had often remarked that I had a vivid imagination, but this was something else. And how could I imagine a word that I'd never even heard before? Necromancy. I didn't have a clue what it meant, unless perhaps it had something to do with necrophilia. Uncle Jack had explained that word to me a while back when it came up on a TV crime programme (Uncle Jack loved crime programmes, especially ones to do with forensics, and the more lurid the better; Dad, predictably, despised them – too artistic, I suppose). Necrophilia was having sex with dead people. Uncle Jack hadn't put it quite that crudely – but that's what it came down to. It was time to do a little research.

I switched on my computer and watched it boot. I opened the internet connection, typed the word 'necromancy' in the search engine window and clicked. At once a list of sites appeared. Just the first ten – ten of 181,000! It was a popular subject all right. I called up the first site – an encyclopaedia – figuring a definition would be a good place to start. 'Necromancy,' I read, 'is a special form of divination or prophecy by the evocation of the dead.' Hmm, not exactly necrophilia then, though still to do with dead people. The word was derived from the Greek *nekros*, meaning dead, and *manteia*, divination. In the past it had sometimes also been referred to as nigromancy (from *niger*, meaning black), suggesting black magic or black art.

They practise the Black Art.

The words seemed to sound themselves out in the air around me, which had a sudden chill. I read on. 'The practice of necromancy supposes belief in the survival of the soul after death, the possession of a superior knowledge by the disembodied spirit, and the possibility of communication between the living and the dead.'

I started as, through the words on the screen, a boy's

face appeared, framed by a monk's cowl. It was the same face I'd seen before – spectrally pale with deep, searching brown eyes. And I knew instinctively that it was Brother Boniface. His lips moved, mouthing words that I strained to hear. I leaned closer to the screen, so close that my eyes were almost touching the glass. But my gaze caught only my own reflection. The vision vanished as suddenly as it had come. I rested my forehead against the screen and sighed with exasperation. I felt edgy, disappointed, totally drained.

It was pointless talking to Dad about it. The mere mention of divination or prophecy would have him snorting with derision. Uncle Jack would be interested, but only in a superficial way – for what it could give him as a kind of beyond-the-grave tipster. And I knew there was a lot more to it than that. I hadn't been trying to evoke the dead; Brother Boniface was trying to communicate with *me*, like he had something to tell. It was like prophecy in reverse: not foretelling the future but revealing the past. I just didn't know how to explain what was happening and it was really starting to disturb me. It was like I was losing control, being taken over in some way, haunted, possessed. Could it be that it was simply my mind playing elaborate tricks? Maybe it was all part of the trauma I'd been going through – a side effect of my grief, like Dad had suggested to the doctor. Or maybe it was something worse. I mean, I was seeing things, wasn't I? The way mad people did. What if I was slipping into madness? That possibility was much more scary than any of the things I was seeing. They didn't scare me at all. Even if Brother Boniface was a ghost, I knew he meant me no harm.

No, I wouldn't speak to Dad or Uncle Jack. I'd talk to Father Christopher, I decided, after the service on Sunday. Perhaps he could shed some more light on this whole necromancy thing. Before shutting down the computer, I'd discovered from my web surfing that necromancy was mentioned in the Bible, in the Book of Kings – something to do with the Witch of Endor. I could use that as a way of broaching the subject of this whole Boniface business.

I made the right decision about not talking to Dad. Well, not that day anyway. He was in a foul mood. Wagstaff had called an impromptu press conference for that afternoon at the abbey site. A skeleton had been found beneath the altar and Wagstaff was convinced it belonged to Boniface. His theory was that it had become separated from the head during the initial digging. He insisted that Dad should be present to give an update on his progress with the reconstruction of the skull.

'I'd be making a damned sight more progress if that fool would let me get on with my work and stop involving me in his stupid publicity stunts,' Dad complained to me bitterly.

I asked him if I could go with him to the abbey.

He looked at me, surprised, though not displeased. 'Why would you want to do that?' he queried.

I shrugged. 'Something to do,' I said. The truth was I didn't know exactly why I wanted to go; the idea had just suddenly come to me. It was like Boniface was inside my head, calling to me – and I couldn't say no. And I could rationalize it too. Well, a trip to the place where the novice had lived and where his skull had been found – and maybe now his skeleton too – would surely help in getting a sense of what sort of person he had been. Not that Dad would understand that – or even consider it relevant really. Reconstructing Boniface was a clinical scientific exercise to him – a calculation of muscles, glands and bones. Character didn't come into it. But that was what made the flesh come to life, wasn't it: in a smile, a frown?

It was a two-hour drive from where we lived to the abbey and most of it passed in silence. We didn't find it easy to talk to one another at the best of times, and today definitely wasn't one of those. Dad was sullen and uncommunicative, resenting the impending ordeal of having to bow to Wagstaff and answer press questions, and I was deep in my own concerns. I did consider, once or twice, mentioning the strange experiences I'd been having, but I couldn't quite bring myself to do it. I just couldn't face the inevitable disapproval or dismissal. So I said nothing.

The abbey was set in the middle of the countryside and we had to wind our way through narrow lanes to reach it. I caught sight of it about a mile away, as we drove down a steep hill. In the grey winter's light it looked sort of desolate and lonely. I wondered how it had looked back in Boniface's day, when it was a working monastery and not a ruin, though it hadn't exactly been new even then. The first monastic buildings, Dad told me in one of his rare moments of speech on the way down, had been erected in the thirteenth century, well over a hundred years before Boniface had entered the place. How would he have felt that first day, I wondered, as he approached the abbey on horseback or in some kind of carriage? His whole life had been about to change for ever, his childhood and his family left behind. How would I have felt? Apprehensive certainly, miserable probably – and angry? If my parents had done that to me, I'd have been angry all right, but things were different then, weren't they? People had different beliefs and aspirations. Maybe he'd always wanted to be a monk; maybe he was fulfilling his ambition. For all I knew his heart might have been racing with excitement, the way mine was now as we drove into the abbey car park. At last

I was entering Boniface's world. I was going to walk on the stones and pathways that he had walked . . .

Dad went off to find Wagstaff, and I headed for the abbey site. I wandered by walls of damp grey stone, furred green with moss or speckled white with age. There were small notices throughout the ruins bearing the names of the rooms and details of what they had been used for: cellarium (the abbey storehouse); reredorter (the toilet block); refectory (the dining room); the chapter house (meeting place), where the monks gathered each morning apparently, to discuss monastic affairs; the calefactory (warming room) with its large double fireplace – the only source of heating in the whole abbey apart from in the infirmary (the sick room) and the novices' room.

I stepped through an archway into the novices' room. It was the best-preserved room in the whole place and a breathtaking sight with its beautiful, vaulted ceiling, held up by elegant round pillars that sprouted giant spiders' legs of yellow stone. I went and stood by the fireplace, trying to imagine Brother Boniface sheltering here on a cold winter's day, like today, thawing out his frozen hands before the leaping flames. For an instant I even thought I could see him here, standing in front of the fire with a friend, another novice, at his side, talking in whispers, but when I blinked, there was nothing there but the worn-out stone of the old hearth.

Birds flocked suddenly by the glassless window in a rush of black and grey, their cries a desolate ululation. My excitement had all gone now and I felt very lonely and sad. I'd come here hoping to find some sign of life, but all I'd found was a deeper sense of death. Boniface was gone – just as Mum was – extinguished, lost for ever like those long-dead abbots buried in the chapter house. At least they had some kind of memorial, a grave, a headstone; all Mum had was a plastic urn on a shelf in my bedroom – and Boniface didn't even have that. All that remained of him was that empty skull on a plinth in Dad's workshop. As I sat in the bleak chapter house, staring at the shell of the ancient ruined edifice, it seemed suddenly like a metaphor for my own life since Mum had died – crumbling, caved in, purposeless.

After a while I walked out into the cloisters. A jet flashed over in a rumble of silver, odd and anachronistic in this ancient, primitive place. There were more jarring notes from the present too: the clunk and chink of scaffolding poles which Wagstaff's workmen were erecting in the church, in preparation, apparently, for further excavations. As I entered the church, a scaffolding pole clanged to the ground and a workman swore loudly, rupturing, momentarily, the peaceful sanctity of the place.

The church was an awesome building, huge in length

and height, the heart of the monastery. I felt tiny and insignificant as I stood beneath the massive 'perpendicular window' of the east front, gazing up the nave, with its impressive stone bays, past the choir, where the monks would have sat, and on to the presbytery, where the remains of the high altar still stood, surrounded now by planks of wood, trenches and scatterings of earth from the excavation. What a magnificent sight it must have been in Brother Boniface's time, I thought, when the roof was intact and the stonework clean and uncracked. Even in its ruined state, it retained an imposing atmosphere of power and holiness.

I felt overwhelmed and kind of dizzy so I sat on the stone bench of the choir and looked across at the benches opposite. Above them I could see traces of the skulls that had been carved in a line along the stonework and I thought about Brother Boniface. It was not the most comforting of sights, and this was not the most comfortable of seats. And to think they had had to sit here eight times a day (so the notice at my side informed me) for eight different services! I closed my eyes, trying to shut out the noise of the workmen and let my thoughts and imagination take me back into the past.

The bones are false, the indulgences worthless.

Foul deeds . . . murder.

Necromancy. The Black Art.

The words swirled in my head and I couldn't tell whether someone was really speaking them or whether they were the flesh of my thoughts. I felt myself swaying as the words formed themselves into a tuneless, unintelligible chant, which gradually became music: voices singing – male voices intoning plainsong in unison, the sound full and resonant in the high-ceilinged church. '*Kyrie Eleison. Christe Eleison.*' I felt like I was living in two worlds at the same time.

I opened my eyes to see rows of black-robed monks sitting in candlelight where there had been empty stone and daylight just a moment before.

'Listen,' a voice whispered. And again, more urgently, 'Listen!'

I found myself looking into the deep brown eyes of a novice monk. Brother Boniface spoke again, his eyes drawing me in, taking possession, and this time I had no trouble hearing. 'Look, listen.'

I felt myself falling, but struggled against it.

'You OK, son?' I looked up into a frowning, weather-beaten face topped by a yellow hard hat. 'You shouldn't really be in here while this work's going on.'

'I'm with my dad,' I said woozily. 'He's talking to Dr Wagstaff.'

'Ah, Wagstaff.' The man nodded. 'You shouldn't really be in here all the same. It's not safe.'

'No, right,' I muttered. I took a deep breath and forced myself to stand up. It was one of the hardest things I'd ever done. Every part of my body felt like solid concrete.

'Are you sure you're OK?' the man asked again.

'Yeah.' I nodded.

The man appraised me, unconvinced. 'The quickest way out's there, through the sacristy,' he said, pointing. 'I think you could do with some fresh air.'

'Yeah, thanks.' I nodded again. I walked slowly towards the doorway and into a small anteroom – the sacristy presumably. It was empty; there wasn't even a door. And yet . . . Images started to form in my head – a wooden table, stalls, an open cupboard full of metal cups and plates, communion vessels . . . Two figures talking.

This is the Devil's House.

You know too much, and knowledge is a dangerous, dangerous thing.

My body started to shake and I couldn't control it. I had a sudden feeling of terror: something bad, something terrible had happened here. Or was going to happen? I was slipping between two worlds again. I had to get out of this room before I lost my grip entirely. The voices were so loud, so insistent, pulling me in. I put my hands over my ears and stumbled towards the archway that would lead me out into the cloisters.

I cannot allow you to go.

I was at the archway now: just one more step and I'd be through. I lifted my foot . . . and my head exploded. Consciousness drained from me like blood from a deep wound. I felt myself falling, falling, and fading until I was as empty as a blank page upon which another's story could be written.

PART TWO

CHAPTER 5

The abbot collapsed during Vespers.

He was an elderly man but had always enjoyed good health. During his time at the abbey he had seen many members of the community fall prey to plague and the dreaded sweating sickness, but he himself had remained healthy. Indeed, the analogy between spiritual purity and bodily health was one he was fond of drawing at chapter-house meetings. Thomas had heard him use it in the few weeks he had been at the abbey. There was an air of impregnability about Abbot Eidric, which made his sudden collapse all the more shocking to all who witnessed it. One moment he was leading the responses, the next he was tilting forward over his prayer stool and crashing to the stone floor, hands flailing helplessly from the arms of his habit.

Brother Silvius, the infirmarian, and his assistant,

Brother Dominic, moved quickly to attend the fallen abbot, who was trembling and appeared to be in considerable pain, his hands clutching at his stomach. Carefully the brothers carried him out of the draughty church to the infirmary.

The next morning in the chapter house, after the customary prayers and reading from the Rule of Benedict, the abbot's second in command, Prior Gregory, informed the brethren that Abbot Eidric was seriously ill, though Brother Silvius had been unable as yet to determine what the ailment was. The infirmarian, he said, had treated his patient with an infusion of quince and comfrey and had applied herbal poultices to the abbot's feverish brow, but with no apparent effect.

'We must all say prayers for our Father Abbot. His health is in God's hands, though Brother Silvius will continue to do all he can, I am sure, to aid his recovery. May the Lord sustain and strengthen him in his time of trial.' The prior coughed dryly and pulled at his habit before continuing. 'During the abbot's indisposition, it falls to me to oversee the abbey's affairs. I shall take up residence temporarily in the abbot's lodgings and would ask you all to bring any matters of business to me there.' He nodded at a tall, lean monk with shrewd dark eyes, Brother Alban, who doubled as the abbey treasurer and cellarer, responsible for the monastery's stores and supplies. 'Brother Alban, I would speak with you presently at the conclusion of our gathering.' Brother Alban bowed his head slightly in acquiescence. He was not a man, as Thomas had learned already, given to expansive words or gestures.

Sitting in the cloisters later that afternoon, Thomas found his concentration wavering from the guide to novices on which his thoughts were supposed to be concentrating. It was hard to focus on books when so much was happening in the world immediately around him. He had not known exactly what to expect when entering, with some trepidation, the Benedictine house of Maundle Abbey, but the assumption he had had was that it would be a place of quiet and calm – to a degree of dullness even – and so it had appeared on that first day when Father Eidric had received him into the order.

Thomas had taken to the abbot immediately. He had an aura of absolute authority, but of grace and generosity too. From the start he had made Thomas feel completely welcome, treating him with such kindness and consideration it was almost as if he were the most important member of the abbey, not its newest and lowliest recruit. 'You could have no better mentor than Brother Martin,' he told Thomas, 'but the door to my lodgings is ever open should you have need of succour or guidance.'

Thomas found these words of great comfort that first difficult probationary week, when he was lodged in the guesthouse outside the main monastic buildings. He missed his home – in particular his mother – and lying in the dark at night, alone, he could not help but weep silently into his bolster. Such a reaction was normal, Brother Martin assured him on one of his frequent visits to the guesthouse. Sacrificing your life to God was no easy choice and nor should it be. With his sallow, pockmarked complexion and coarse skin, the novice master might have cut a rather menacing figure were it not for the generous good humour of his eyes, which quickly put strangers at ease. Thomas had warmed to him at once, just as he had to Father Eidric.

If his conversations with Brother Martin and Father Eidric in those first days had led Thomas to believe that the monastery was a place of dedicated service and tranquillity, he'd been quickly disabused of the notion. On the very day he was accepted into the monastery, news had come that Maundle's most prized relic, the right hand of its founder, St Geronimus the Venerable, had been officially authenticated by the Pope. Abbot Eidric had made the announcement at chapter that day, along with his decision that the relic was to be housed at the spiritual heart of the monastery in the foundation stone of a new high altar, the building of which would entail major alterations to the church's presbytery.

This, Thomas quickly realized, was not a decision that received universal favour. Indeed, it provoked open discord among some of the senior brothers – in particular Prior Gregory, Brother Alban and the sacristan, Brother Symeon – who objected not to the building works, but to the positioning of the relic.

'Surely the holy relic should be put on display in a prominent position,' Brother Symeon argued, 'where it may inspire hearts and minds to prayer and penitence.'

Brother Alban agreed, adding that authenticated holy relics were of huge financial as well as spiritual value, for they attracted pilgrims, and pilgrims brought gifts and money. Like many monasteries around the country, Maundle Abbey was in a parlous state, he pointed out; numbers had dwindled alarmingly over the past decades, as had its list of benefactors.

'A relic such as the hand of Saint Geronimus offers a precious lifeline,' suggested Prior Gregory. 'But it needs to be put where people can see it and, preferably, touch it. Most abbeys display their relics in special reliquaries that are themselves great treasures. Would it not be a wasted opportunity to bury the sacred hand beneath an altar, however worthy the intention?'

But in the end it was the abbot's decision that held sway, for it was he who was in charge. At least he had been, until yesterday evening. Now, Thomas reflected, nothing was certain. It seemed that the abbot might not have long to live. For the moment Prior Gregory was in command, and that disconcerted Thomas. It wasn't something he'd confess to anyone else and he felt guilty even thinking it, but he didn't like the prior. Where Abbot Eidric gave off an aura of piety and compassion, Prior Gregory seemed cold and aloof. He reminded Thomas more of his father's merchant acquaintances than a holy father. He knew it was wrong of him to have these feelings, for Prior Gregory demanded his respect – he had served the order faithfully for many years, and what right did he, Thomas, a mere novice of a fortnight, have to doubt him?

'Idling, Thomas?'

The voice of the novice master, Brother Martin, brought Thomas quickly from his reverie.

'I was . . . reflecting,' Thomas offered unconvincingly.

'Reflecting upon the wise words of Brother Stephen, I hope. Not some daydream of your own fancy.' Brother Martin spoke sternly, but there was, as ever, a smile in his light blue eyes.

The young novice looked down at his book. 'Indeed, Brother Stephen is so wise,' he said at last, 'that he makes me feel a fool. I wonder how I shall ever be able to live up to his reverence.'

'Ah, Thomas. Do not forget, Brother Stephen was himself a novice once. None of us is born wise; it is a lesson we learn if we trust in God – and our teachers.'

Thomas coloured, remembering his thoughts about Brother Gregory. He felt as if Brother Martin could see within him and was admonishing him.

'I will try my best,' he said.

Brother Martin hitched up his habit and sat down on the stone bench beside his pupil.

'You have come at a testing time, Thomas. The abbot's illness is very troubling to us all.'

'Will Abbot Eidric die?' Thomas asked.

'We shall all die, Thomas, when it is our time. For now we must draw deep of our faith and pray for our Father Abbot and for guidance – young and' – he hesitated with a brief smile – '*not* so young alike.'

'My mother often used to speak of the abbot. She said he was a great man, a great teacher. She had read some of his books.'

The novice master nodded. 'Your mother speaks well.'

Speaking about his mother and receiving this approval for her from the monk he most admired filled Thomas with a sudden sense of well-being that not even the chilly breeze blowing through the open cloisters could dispel.

For a while the novice and his master sat in silent contemplation. Brother Martin looked out at the patch of green grass at the centre of the cloisters, running his hand over the corner pillars with their pattern of a crown topped by small, intricate spirals as if he were trying to touch a memory. Then he said wistfully, 'Abbot Eidric was my novice master when I came here many years ago. We all loved and respected him, as I still do today. You do not meet men of that quality often.'

Thomas looked at his master, trying to imagine him as a boy.

Brother Martin smiled. 'Yes, Thomas, I was a boy like you once. Truly. Though I see in your eyes you find it hard to believe.'

The keenness of his observation flustered Thomas. 'No, no, I—'

Brother Martin laughed softly. 'Don't worry, Thomas, I sometimes find it hard to believe myself.'

His words were met by the sound of tutting nearby. It was Brother Symeon, the sacristan, walking towards them from the church. 'I should have thought that there were better lessons to be taught than laughter in the cloisters, Brother,' he intoned censoriously. 'This is a place for silence and holy contemplation, not frivolity and jesting. Perhaps you have forgotten Saint Benedict's condemnation of idle words that move to laughter.'

Brother Martin bowed to his superior. 'I apologize, Brother. You are right. The cloister is no place for laughter.' He stood up and looked the sacristan in the eye. 'We were talking of Father Abbot, in happier days.'

'Hmm.' The sacristan sniffed.

Thomas glanced at the sacristan, with his round pale face and small brown eyes like sultanas. No, he could not imagine the sacristan laughing; he had yet to see him smile. His habitual expression was one of irritated disapproval, as if he were walking too close to the reredorter. His skin was paler than that of most of the other monks because he spent so much of his time inside the church. It was his duty to look after the vestments, robes and cloths used in the services, as well as the holy vessels and relics. It was no secret that he felt the abbey's most precious relic, the hand of St Geronimus, should be under his guardianship and not buried beneath the altar. Perhaps now, Thomas mused, if the abbot were to die, he would get his way.

There was no time for further speculation, however, as at that moment the bell started ringing for Vespers.

'Liam!' The voice comes from far, far above me, as if I were at the bottom of a deep pit. Where am I? Have I fallen? 'Liam!' The same voice again, muffled, like the touch of a fingernail on numbed skin. The voice so familiar yet I can't place it.

I'm floating, boneless, skinless, without head or body. I am I and not I. The voice fades further and further until it is no more than a rustling of breeze through the leaves of a tree.

I am he.

I am we.

Chapter 6

Thomas found it difficult to sleep that night. Usually he was so tired after the day's exertions that sleep came easily, and these hours between the last service of the evening, Compline, and the first of the new day, Matins, were those in which he slept most heavily. But not tonight. His coarse woollen tunic chafed, the rich custardy dowcett dish he'd been served at supper sat uncomfortably in his stomach, the steady snoring of Brother Dominic irked his ears, but most of all he felt homesick. It was hard being completely cut off from the world that had been yours your whole life. This place, this life, was so different from what he'd known before. For a start, he was the only non-adult, with the exception of the one other novice, a strange, simple fellow named Ambrose, whose age was difficult to judge. He was hardly a soulmate in any case.

Thomas tossed and turned on his straw mattress, staring at the plain brown cloth partition that separated him on each side from the other monks. He was glad of the candle-lamps that burned in the dormitory all through the night. If he had to lie sleepless, he preferred that it should not be in pitch black. He'd never liked complete darkness. As a small child he'd often had nightmares and woken sweating and screaming to be soothed back to sleep by his mother's cool hands and sweet singing. How he could have done with them tonight. But his mother was not here and never would be. That part of his life was gone for ever. The Church was his mother – and his father – now.

He thought about Brother Stephen and his cure for insomnia. Look at your coarse woollen blanket and bed-covers and compare your bed to the grave, just as if you were entering it for burial – that was his advice. Failing that, say the Athanasian Creed seven times, or the Seven Penitential Psalms, and you will fall asleep. He might be right, but Thomas couldn't yet recite *one* of the Penitential Psalms, never mind all seven. He was no Latin scholar like his mother was.

It was his mother he missed most of all. He and his older brother, Giles, had never been very close, and he knew Giles wouldn't miss him. They hadn't had much in common, except being of the same flesh and blood. He could say the same of his father too, really. That day, when his parents had brought him to the abbey, his father had been so impatient to be away, to return to his precious business, that he could barely bring himself to say goodbye. Thomas had sensed that he was actually quite pleased to get him off his hands. It was one less distraction from the vital and all-consuming matter of making money – quite literally too, as his most valued and important client was the York Mint.

But his mother would miss him. He was sure of that. She would miss talking to him about books and art and devotional matters. She would miss the evenings playing chess in the parlour by the light of the fire and the simple beeswax candles that filled the room with a beautiful honeyed fragrance, the afternoon walks on the wild moor, Sunday mornings sitting beside one another in church, sharing their faith . . . Just thinking of these things made his heart ache. He knew that what he was doing would make his mother proud. As much as she loved him and would miss him, she believed that this was the right course for him. In her eyes – and, yes, in his too – there was no greater vocation than devoting yourself to the service of God. But that didn't make it easy – especially at times like this, lying sleepless in the pungent, smoky darkness, apart from the one you loved most of all in the world . . .

A shrill cry brought him sharply to his senses. It sounded like the yell of someone in deep pain. He sat up and listened. All was silent except for Brother Dominic's snoring and the somnolent breathing of the other monks in the dormitory. No one else, it seemed, had been disturbed. Perhaps it had been a fox or a screech owl. There was plenty of wildlife in the vicinity of the monastery. And yet it had sounded so human and so distressing. It made him think of Father Eidric. He prayed the abbot would recover.

There was no way he could sleep now and he lay awake until the call to Matins.

CHAPTER 7

On the third day after his collapse, the abbot's condition improved. Brother Silvius reported that he was no longer vomiting and shaking and had even sat up briefly, though he was still very weak and pale. Spirits were raised throughout the community and prayers of thanksgiving offered at all the services that day. Sadly, however, the abbot's recovery was short-lived. The following day saw his condition worsen and he had soon lapsed into a coma. Brother Silvius resorted to blood-letting to try to restore the abbot to health, but without success. Still baffled by the cause of the ailment, Brother Silvius decided to consult a higher authority and sent one of the infirmary servants to town to seek the help of a respected local physician called Matthew Cundulus.

In the meantime Brother Gregory ruled the abbey. His

chapter meetings were more business-like than Abbot Eidric's and his style of leadership ruthless. In the first week of his rule there were three beatings. Thomas found each of these disturbing, but the one given to his fellow novice, Ambrose, who had been accused of stealing bread from the kitchen, shocked him greatly. It didn't seem such a terrible crime to Thomas – there was always bread left over anyway – but Brother Gregory said that stealing was a mortal sin and that Ambrose must be made an example of. His choice of reading in chapter that day was Chapter 6 of the Rule of St Benedict, concerning the correction of young novices. Ambrose's cloak and tunic were stripped down to the waist and, in front of the whole order, his bare back was beaten with a birch rod until it was raw and bloody. As novice master, Brother Martin had to administer the beating. He protested to the prior, but was quickly reminded of his duty of obedience, as set out in Chapter 7 of the Rule, and had no choice but to carry out the punishment. With each strike he grimaced at Ambrose's yelps of pain and Thomas could see how much the action grieved him. By contrast Brother Gregory showed no emotion at all, while Brother Symeon, sitting at his side, looked on with a smile of gloating satisfaction.

Thomas thought the whole thing horrible. The chapter house, with its gloom and cold stone benches flanking the graves of former abbots, was his least favourite place in the abbey and at that moment he would rather have been anywhere in the world than there. It was not unusual to be beaten: as young children Thomas and his brother had often received such correction at the hand of their father, but this beating seemed especially cruel. Was not Jesus merciful, the Redeemer of the world? Ambrose was a simple soul, not malicious or unruly. Surely he was not deserving of such harsh chastisement? And to compel Brother Martin, the one who cared most for him, to administer the punishment seemed to Thomas to be truly heartless.

At the end of the meeting Thomas helped Brother Martin take Ambrose to the lavatorium, a stone trough filled with cold water at the south side of the cloisters, where they washed his wounds. Then they went on to the infirmary, where Brother Silvius applied a poultice of herbs mixed with honey from the abbey's own hives to stop the bleeding.

'It's wonderful stuff, honey,' the infirmarian enthused, sniffing his hands, which were lined and rough from years of tending his medicinal herb garden. 'It has considerable palliative powers and greatly reduces the risk of infection.' He licked the end of one calloused finger. 'Tastes good too.'

'But it cannot work miracles,' Brother Martin remarked sadly. 'Our Father Abbot is still no better?'

Brother Silvius shook his large head. 'He breathes just, yet his eyes do not open. I am at a loss, I must confess. We must hope Matthew Cundulus can find some remedy. He is a man of expert knowledge and skill. I know of no better physician.'

Thomas remarked how weary the infirmarian looked and sounded. His complexion, usually so rude and hale, was as pale as Brother Symeon's. Lines of worry scored the corners of his eyes. His back was rounded and hunched as if overburdened by responsibility. For him, this was truly a time of trial.

'I pray this man can save Father Eidric,' sighed Brother Martin. 'I fear for us all if Brother Gregory holds sway much longer.' He breathed deeply. 'It seems he would break us.'

'He'll brook no opposition, that is for sure,' Brother Silvius agreed. 'I did wonder if . . .' He glanced at Thomas as if suddenly registering his presence, and hesitated. Evidently he decided against continuing. 'I must return to my patients,' he said. 'Let young Ambrose remain here for the rest of the day. I shall need to keep an eye on those wounds.'

After High Mass, Thomas sat at a desk in the

scriptorium, practising his copying skills under the watchful eye of Brother Luke, the librarian. As usual, when the bell rang for dinner, he was starving and went quickly to the lavatorium to wash his hands and then on to the refectory, where he took his seat at the table. At home, meal times had been lively, bustling affairs with conversation and laughter. At Maundle Abbey it was very different. No talking was permitted. Simple sign language was used for essential communication – to ask for a dish to be passed, for example – but no words. The only voice heard was that of the monk whose task it was that day to read from a selected sacred book. All through the meal he stood in a raised pulpit and read aloud while his fellow monks ate their dinner. The idea behind this, as Brother Martin had informed Thomas, was that the holy words would feed the minds and hearts of the brothers at the same time as the food filled their stomachs. Today it was Brother Alban's turn, but his reading was far from inspirational. He read from St Paul's letters to the Corinthians as if he were reciting a list of accounts. Thomas found his concentration focused entirely on his food. As usual there was no meat, but there was a thick pottage of oatmeal, vegetables and fish, and fried eggs too. It was plainer cooking than he was used to at home, but at least there was plenty of it.

It was only when he'd finished mopping his dish with his bread and looked up properly for the first time that he registered there was a newcomer facing him on the other side of the U in which the tables were arranged. He appeared to be about the same age as Thomas and was dressed in a novice's habit. Thomas took in the deep-set quizzical eyes and pale face speckled with freckles. He was baffled. The other novices at Maundle Abbey were all grown men, so who could this be? Was he new to the order? If so, surely he should be spending his first days in the guesthouse before being admitted to the abbey.

He didn't have to wait long for his curiosity to be satisfied. After lunch Brother Martin summoned him to the parlour and introduced him to the newcomer.

'Thomas, this is Nicholas. He has joined us today at Maundle. I shall leave him to explain the circumstances. Then perhaps you would show him around the abbey until Nones.' Nones was the first service of the afternoon, the sixth of the day.

'Of course,' Thomas agreed, bowing his head politely.

Nicholas, Thomas soon discovered, was an oblate like him. His parents had given him into the service of nearby Larksby Abbey just days before Thomas had entered Maundle. Larksby was smaller than Maundle and only fifteen monks lived there. It had already been struggling to survive when, just two days previously, a catastrophic fire had swept through the abbey, destroying most of the buildings and killing five of the brothers. Those left were mainly old or infirm and had neither the energy nor the resources to think of rebuilding the community. Instead they had decided to disband and seek refuge among neighbouring Benedictine houses. Brother Gregory had agreed to take in Nicholas, Larksby's only novice, on condition that he brought with him Larksby's most valued treasure: a magnificent reliquary fashioned in crystal and silver gilt, containing a leg bone of St Anselm.

'Your abbot was a friend of Abbot William,' Nicholas said. 'He always spoke very highly of him. I am sorry to hear that he is ill.'

'Yes, it is a sad time for all of us,' Thomas agreed, recalling momentarily the abbot's welcoming face the day his parents had delivered him to the abbey.

Nicholas looked down, revealing a frizz of fair hair around his tonsure. 'At least he lives still,' he said quietly. 'Father William died in the fire.'

Chapter 8

Thomas and Nicholas quickly became friends. One of the things that Thomas had found hardest about settling in to life at Maundle was the absence of anyone else of his own age with whom to share the experience. Nicholas's arrival more than filled that void. Brother Martin even made special arrangements so that Nicholas could sleep in the bed next to Thomas. It was usual practice to separate novices, to lessen the temptation for chattering in the dormitory, where silence was compulsory. These were exceptional circumstances, though – Nicholas had suffered a traumatic event and it was important to make him feel welcomed in his new home.

The two novices had much in common. Nicholas too was a younger son who had been given as an oblate to the abbey by his parents – or rather, his father. He had supplied meat to Larksby Abbey, which no longer farmed animals of its own, and he thought that offering his son as a novice would be a good business move. As Nicholas remarked wryly, it hadn't worked out like that.

As well as having lessons in many different aspects of being a monk from Brother Martin, the boys were given practical tasks each day, working in different parts of the monastery. They were in the infirmary, helping Brother Silvius, on the afternoon Matthew Cundulus finally arrived. It was three days since he had been summoned, but, as he now explained, he had been away in London attending to one of King Henry's most esteemed advisers. It had been a delicate matter, he said, requiring all his skill, but he was pleased to report that the matter had been concluded to everyone's satisfaction. He hoped that this situation might be too.

'Now, lead me to the patient,' he pronounced with a flourish.

Everything about Matthew Cundulus had flourish. He was not at all what Thomas would have imagined. His family's physician had been serious and sombre in dress and manner, but Matthew Cundulus was the opposite. He dressed from head to foot like a dandy. He wore a black velvet hat with a long tail. His doublet was peacock blue, embroidered with silver, with huge padded sleeves and shoulders. It was drawn in tight at the waist and was so short that it barely covered his ample codpiece. His midnight-blue hose clung to his legs like a second skin and his shoes had such long points that they had had to be curled up and attached with thin chains to his shins so that he could walk without tripping over. Thomas had never seen anything like it.

Brother Silvius led the physician to the bed where the abbot lay, still unconscious. Now Matthew Cundulus's manner was entirely changed. He was every bit the expert professional as he examined the abbot with various instruments he produced from his large leather bag, asking questions as he did so. He wanted to know in detail about the abbot's illness and its stages. Brother Silvius informed him of the abbot's collapse, of the early vomiting and diarrhoea, the brief recovery, followed by convulsions and then coma.

'His skin is very cold – and yellow,' the physician remarked. 'Has he passed urine recently?'

Brother Silvius shook his head. 'Not for days.'

Matthew Cundulus stood up straight and stared at his patient with his hands on his hips. 'How long after he last ate was it that he fell ill?' he asked.

Brother Silvius looked surprised by the question. He thought for a moment. 'About six or seven hours.'

Matthew Cundulus wagged his head musingly, so that his cap slipped forwards. He raised a hand and pushed it back. 'I require a tour of your grounds and gardens,' he announced at last. 'I shall need to remove some samples for investigation.'

'Of course,' Brother Silvius agreed. 'But can you help our Father Abbot?'

Matthew Cundulus looked uncharacteristically grave. 'Only God may do that, Brother. I suggest you pray for the abbot's soul, for he is surely very near to his end. I wonder that he has continued so long.'

'But what is the matter with him?'

Matthew Cundulus ran his hand over his cleanly shaven chin. 'I should prefer not to reveal my diagnosis until I have had time to execute certain tests, but . . .' He paused theatrically, glancing around as if confirming that he had a full audience before continuing.

'Yes?' Brother Silvius prompted. There was a hush as if the whole room were holding its breath.

Matthew Cundulus narrowed his eyes, and with impressive gravitas said, 'It is my considered belief, Brother, that Abbot Eidric's condition has not been induced by natural causes.'

I often think about it – that last day. And of course I often wonder what if . . . What if I'd been ill and hadn't gone to school? What if Dad had been off at some site somewhere and using the car? What if the fan-belt had snapped instead of just slipping and Mum hadn't been able to drive the car? What if whatever happened to make her lose control and crash the car that day hadn't happened? What if the wall she smashed into had been made of rubber, not concrete? What if . . . ? I can carry on like for hours, but it won't bring her back.

I was playing football when it happened, an after-school team practice preparing for a big cup match the following Saturday. McIntyre, our coach, put us through our paces – running round the pitch five times and then sprinting in pairs before we got to put foot to ball. 'I'm dead,' I said to my mate Zeddy. I can hear myself saying it now, head thrown back, gasping. 'I'm dead.' Well, I wasn't – but Mum was.

I got the news on the bus on the way home, my mobile ringing out 'I Heard It Through the Grapevine', which I'd just downloaded the night before. It was Dad, which surprised me because he never rang my mobile. I don't remember exactly what he said, just the tone of his voice – unusually urgent and intense. He told me Mum had had a serious car accident and had been taken to hospital. He'd tell me more when I got home.

Mum was already dead, I found out later, before they got her to hospital. She was barely alive when the ambulance arrived and never regained consciousness. But what was she thinking about, I often wonder, in those seconds when the car was careering towards that concrete wall? Did any thought of me flash through her mind in those final moments? Did she suffer at all before she died? There aren't any answers, I know, but it doesn't stop me wondering.

I guess I'll always wonder.

CHAPTER 9

Thomas was woken by a scream. He sat up in bed, startled and gasping. His heart was beating fast and his body was shaking. He closed his eyes and tried to steady his breathing. The scream had been part of his dream but that did not make it any less terrifying, because it had been his mother who had been screaming. She had been falling through a window, glass smashing around her. It seemed so real, even now that Thomas was awake, that it took him some time to convince himself that it had only been a dream.

When he felt calmer, he got up and lifted the curtain that separated his bed from Nicholas's. His fellow novice was fast asleep, barely visible beneath the mound of woollen bedcover and robe. The dormitory resonated with the sounds of sleeping. As before, it seemed that the scream had been audible to Thomas alone.

He lay back down on his bed and listened to the night. Beyond the snores and stentorian breathing of the brethren was another more soothing sound – the gentle shushing of running water in the river behind the abbey. It was a beautiful calming sound. All monasteries were built near rivers, for fresh water was essential to any community. But its significance was not limited to bodily sustenance, washing and cooking; a river was deeply spiritual too. Lying in the dark, Thomas felt the lulling sound wash over and refresh him.

He considered the events of the day. And what a momentous day it had been! Matthew Cundulus's dramatic pronouncement had brought a gasp from the infirmarian and his assistant – as Thomas was sure the physician had intended. But what had he meant by 'not induced by natural causes'? When pressed by Brother Silvius, he would say no more. Instead he had enquired of the infirmarian as to what plants and herbs he grew, and then asked to be shown the gardens.

'I would not take up your valuable time, Brother,' he had said. Then, acknowledging Thomas's presence for the first time, he added, 'Perhaps you could spare the boy to be my guide.'

So it was that Thomas had spent the next hour with the distinguished doctor. They walked around the kitchen garden, where two monks were busy hoeing, and Brother Silvius's own small and neat herb garden, which he tended himself with the help of one of the abbey servants. Matthew Cundulus stood beneath the intricate entrance arch with his arms folded.

'What do you see, boy?' he asked Thomas grandly.

'Plants, sir. Herbs.'

'Precisely. Plants, herbs.' Matthew Cundulus was evidently unimpressed. 'You might suppose, looking at this, that medicine was simply a glorified form of gardening, not the learned science that it should be. We live in a world of amateurism and folk remedies. Where mustard and garlic are prescribed for plague and nettles for insomnia. Where a spider wrapped in a raisin is considered a cure for ague and a bag of buttercups worn round the neck will stave off insanity. Ridiculous, isn't it? Laughable. But such nonsense is what we physicians must counter every day. It is worse than any disease I know.'

As they walked around the infirmarian's garden, Matthew Cundulus pointed, pouted, sniffed and snorted. He introduced Thomas to the lungwort plant, explaining how it received its name from the resemblance of its white-spotted leaves to the human lung, and the blue-flowered borage which, he said with a dismissive laugh, had been given to the Crusaders before leaving England to give them courage. He tasted leaves of horseradish and liquorice and invited Thomas to do the same. And all the time he instructed Thomas to take samples and deposit them carefully in a large leather pouch he had brought for the purpose. Usually he asked for no more than a leaf or the tiniest cutting. But when they reached the parsley, he commanded Thomas to pull out a whole clump.

'It will be of more use to me than anyone here,' he said.

Thomas was intrigued. 'Why is that, sir? What special medicinal properties does it hold?'

'Why, none, boy. It's an aphrodisiac, excellent for the enhancement of sexual performance. Wasted on you monks.' He glanced down at his codpiece and laughed heartily, while Thomas blushed to the roots.

It did seem to Thomas, however, that despite his apparent good humour, Matthew Cundulus was not entirely happy with what he had discovered in the gardens. As he followed Thomas from the abbey buildings and out into the busy great court where his horse was tethered, the doctor was uncharacteristically quiet and pensive. Perhaps he was disheartened, Thomas thought, by his inability to help the abbot. He did not have the air of a man who was accustomed to failure.

The doctor's taciturnity did not last long. As they approached the stables, he stopped suddenly and, with a flourish of his puffed sleeve, ordered Thomas to do likewise. Then, beckoning to him, he marched towards a tall oak tree. With some difficulty, due to the tightness of his doublet and hose, Matthew Cundulus went down on his haunches in order to better study the foot of the tree or, more explicitly, what else was growing there.

'Now that is interesting,' he murmured as Thomas arrived beside him. 'What do you see there, boy?'

Thomas looked. 'Mushrooms, sir.'

'Yes, mushrooms. But not any old mushrooms, unless I am much mistaken – which would be a very rare occurrence indeed.' Matthew Cundulus was his blustery self-confident self once more.

Thomas gazed at the mushrooms. They were quite small and very white, with a kind of veil around the stem. 'What is special about these mushrooms, sir?' he asked.

'See those white gills? See the way they are detached from the stalk? I would say they were *Amanita bisporigera*. Death's Angel.' He produced a silk kerchief from his doublet, carefully picked one of the mushrooms and put it in the pouch. Then he fixed on Thomas a stare of unexpected intensity. 'This is our secret, boy. Breathe not a word to anyone until I have completed my examinations. These are dangerous times and disclosures to the wrong ears may be a very dangerous thing indeed. You mark my meaning?'

Lying on his mattress, Thomas thought about the physician's warning. He had not really comprehended it at the time and nor did he now. What danger was he talking about? Surely there could be no danger here in a monastery. This was a sanctuary, a holy place, away from all the troubles and strife of the outside world. There could be no safer place than this, could there? Thomas's mind returned again to Matthew Cundulus's pronouncement about Abbot Eidric's condition. What had he meant by it? That the abbot had been the victim of some unfortunate accident? Surely not that someone had attempted deliberately to kill him? Who could have done such a thing? The monks were men of God; to take a life, and such an esteemed life, would be a negation of everything the order stood for. Such an act would damn the perpetrator for eternity. Thomas shivered at the thought. He felt suddenly vulnerable and alone. He wished Matthew Cundulus hadn't included him in his confidence. It felt wrong to withhold knowledge from his brethren. It was like betraying his own family.

He thought of home – of his dark empty room with its two unoccupied beds, of the blue wall-hangings, the dark chest with its carved beasts, the comforting animal skulls . . . How he wished he had them with him now. He pictured his mother and father in their nightcaps and gowns, sleeping in their chamber, their little dog, Lot, curled up at the foot of the bed. How he missed them all. He wanted to make them proud, to live his life doing God's bidding and in his service, but it was hard – hard to be away from everything he knew and loved, even with the company of a friend like Nicholas.

Breathe not a word, Matthew Cundulus had said. *These are dangerous times*. But his gaze had no longer been fixed on Thomas; it had moved beyond. Then he'd frowned.

'What in Jehovah's name is he doing here?' His frown had deepened. 'Now that is interesting. Very interesting.'

Thomas had turned and taken in the crowded scene of pilgrims, servants, monks and townsfolk. There had been no way of knowing who the doctor had been talking about and he had had no chance to enquire, for Matthew Cundulus was already on his way to the stables. Minutes later he had mounted up and, with a wink to Thomas and a raise of one beringed finger to his lips, he had been on his way.

The day after Mum's accident there was a ring at the door. I was still groggy from the sedatives I'd been given the evening before to try to calm me and help me sleep. I hadn't really been able to take it all in, to be honest. My mind still expected Mum to appear – and I think that was what was in my head when I opened the front door: that she'd be there, doing that jangling thing she did with the car keys when she was feeling impatient. 'You took your time,' she'd tut, and march past me into the house. But of course it wasn't Mum; it was a stranger with a big cellophane-wrapped package of white roses in his arms. 'Interflora delivery for Laura Marshall,' he declared cheerily, handing them over. I looked at him blankly.

He gave me a quizzical stare. 'Laura Marshall does live here, doesn't she?' he asked.

I started to nod, then froze. I swallowed, trying to hold back my tears. I shook my head. 'She's dead,' I croaked.

I thought the flowers had been sent by some family friend in sympathy (that's what people did, wasn't it, when somebody died – they sent flowers), but when I opened the small envelope attached and took out the card, I discovered they were from Dad. I read the message written there, hand-printed by some disinterested florist, perhaps even by the guy who'd delivered them, and I started to sob and howl: 'Happy anniversary, darling! All my love, Will.'

That day was my mum and dad's fifteenth wedding anniversary.

Chapter 10

Abbot Eidric died during the night. The last rites were administered and he passed away shortly before Matins. He was dressed for burial in a clean tunic and his body laid out on a special stone in the infirmary chapel. All that day at frequent intervals the abbey bells tolled and prayers were uttered.

Towards dusk, the abbot's body was placed in a pine-wood coffin and carried in solemn procession through the cloisters to the church. There, in an atmosphere of smoking candles and incense, the Office of the Dead was recited. Throughout the night, the monks took turns to keep vigil, chanting psalms and offering up prayers. As novices, Thomas and Nicholas were excused this duty, but they volunteered anyway.

Thomas found the ceremonies of the day intensely

affecting. His initial admiration for Abbot Eidric had turned to a deep reverence in the short time he had known him. In addition, the revelations of the day before gave him a heavy sense of involvement in the abbot's fate. The secret he bore hung heavily within him. He half hoped that Brother Silvius might reveal Matthew Cundulus's suspicions to the prior, and relieve Thomas of his burden, but he saw no evidence of it. The infirmarian had been too busy that day for conversation and besides, he had given the doctor his word that he would say nothing until any suspicions were properly confirmed.

Early that morning a Requiem Mass was held for the abbot, led by Prior Gregory, in resplendent white robes to signify the resurrection, and Brother Bernard, the precentor, who had chosen music of which Abbot Eidric was particularly fond. Thomas found the ceremony deeply moving (he had never attended a funeral before) – especially when Prior Gregory blessed the open coffin with incense and holy water to the accompaniment of the monks, singing Psalm 42: '*As the hart panteth after the water brooks, so panteth my soul after thee, o God.*' Closing his eyes momentarily, Thomas felt his soul rise with the music, high into the vaulted beams of the church and beyond, as if transported to Heaven.

At the end of the service, the monks carried the coffin to

the chapter house, where Abbot Eidric was buried alongside his predecessors, returning, as Prior Gregory remarked with uncharacteristic poeticism, 'into the womb of the mother of all'. It was a beautiful phrase, Thomas thought, the maternal sentiments having a particular resonance in his own heart and drawing a comforting cloak, albeit fleetingly, around the terrible circumstances of the abbot's death.

That afternoon Prior Gregory summoned to the abbot's lodgings the senior monks, the obedientiaries: Brother Alban, Brother Symeon, Brother Bernard, Brother Silvius, Brother Luke and Brother Martin – the novice master was giving Thomas and Nicholas a Latin lesson in the novices' room when he was sought out by one of the abbey servants.

'Brother Gregory has wasted no time,' he commented with an ironic smile.

'What do you mean, Father?' Thomas asked.

'I cannot say for sure, but I imagine Brother Gregory's mind is on who will replace Abbot Eidric.'

'Will it be the prior?' Nicholas wondered.

'He would have it so. But it is not that simple.' Brother Martin fingered his silver cross thoughtfully. 'There will be an election. We brothers shall vote in our new abbot. It is our custom, our right and our duty.'

With that he straightened his habit, tightened the cord cincture that belted it and hurried away.

'I think Brother Martin would make a good abbot,' said Nicholas. 'I would vote for him.'

'So would I,' Thomas agreed. Their opinions counted for nothing, he knew, for as they hadn't yet taken their final vows, neither of them would be allowed to vote. He hoped that Brother Martin or Brother Silvius would be elected abbot, but he suspected that it would be Brother Gregory. He prayed that it wouldn't be Brother Symeon, with his sour face and disapproving tongue.

Thomas told Nicholas about his tour round the gardens with Matthew Cundulus. He described the incident with the mushrooms (the physician had warned him to tell no one, but he could not keep it from Nicholas, and besides, he swore him to secrecy). 'Death's Angel, he called them.'

Nicholas shivered. 'What a horrible name,' he said. 'My brother was sick once from eating mushrooms he picked in the woods near our home.'

'My brother Giles did the same,' said Thomas. 'My mother told us never to eat wild mushrooms, but that only made Giles more determined to try.' He shook his head at the memory and the distress caused to his mother. 'He vomited for days. The doctor said he was fortunate not to die.'

'Do you suppose Matthew Cundulus thought those mushrooms had something to do with Abbot Eidric's sickness?' Nicholas mused.

'I don't know.' Thomas shrugged. 'Hopefully we shall soon discover.'

But no word came from Matthew Cundulus that day.

In the evening Brother Gregory was elected the new abbot of Maundle Abbey. The vote was not unanimous, but it was substantial enough. The official inauguration would be made by the bishop on his next visit, when Abbot Gregory, as he was now to be known, would be presented with the ring and crook that went with the office of abbot. A new era had begun at the abbey. Thomas prayed that it would be a period of peace and prosperity – though, as he lay in bed that night, Matthew Cundulus's caution that these were dangerous times sat uncomfortably in his heart.

Mum was cremated. She wasn't religious and Dad certainly wasn't. 'She wouldn't want any fuss,' he said – and, though I knew he was right, it seemed to me like we were failing her somehow, allowing her to slip away to ashes so utterly anonymously. Only Dad and I went to the crematorium. Mum was an only child and had no close relatives, and the only one Dad had, Uncle Jack, was away in Bali. They had a few friends, but Dad said he wanted it to be just the of us. There was no ceremony as such – some registrar g. said a few words and one of Mum's favourite tunes, 'Candle in the Wind' by Elton John, was piped through some speakers as her coffin slid away into the flames and oblivion. I was in a real mess – I couldn't stop crying. Dad, on the other hand, didn't shed a single tear. From the moment those flowers arrived, the roses he'd ordered for their wedding anniversary, he'd been like stone. It was like something had died inside him.

While we stood there, watching the coffin disappear, I had this memory from when I was in primary school, aged about nine or ten. An author – I can't remember what his name was – had come into school for our book week, and he'd given us a talk about writing and his books and stuff. He talked about wishes and what a good starting point they could be for creating stories. He told us to imagine he was our fairy godmother and could grant us one wish, what would we ask for? Well, there were all the usual answers like a million more wishes, a billion pounds, to be a footballer, to have a pony, to fly . . . And then I put up my hand and told him my wish. 'To have a coffin,' I said. The class laughed and the author frowned as if he thought I was crazy. It wasn't that I wanted to be dead, I explained, nothing weird like that. It wasn't an ordinary coffin I

…ed but one of those ancient Egyptian ones like they …d in the British Museum (Dad loved the place and had …aken me there several times), all painted with amazing symbols and hieroglyphs and pictures of insects and animals – and eyes too so that you'd be able to see out when you went into the afterlife. They even had pictures on the inside. That's the kind of coffin I wanted. I told Mum about it when I got home. She smiled sort of sadly and nodded. 'I could do with one of those,' she said. 'You could just lie in it and go to sleep for ever.'

Well, now her wish had come true.

CHAPTER 11

The new abbot's first action was to appoint Brother Alban as prior, which was hardly a surprise as the two already worked so closely together. His next action received a more enthusiastic reaction. At the chapter meeting the next morning, Abbot Gregory declared the day a feast day – an announcement which was greeted with nods and smiles by the brethren, for it meant that a more extensive and appetizing range of culinary fare would grace their table. Brother Alban announced, without any noticeable enthusiasm, that special dishes of pike and salmon would be served, which pleased Thomas as he loved fish. It had often been served at his parents' table.

The two novices spent their morning in the scriptorium with Brother Luke. While Nicholas practised his scribing skills, Thomas, who had shown a flare for illustration, received a lesson in ink-making. Under Brother Luke's critical gaze, Thomas mixed together pulverized oak gold, copperas and gum arabic with water to produce ink, taking care to blend the ingredients in the right proportions so that the ink would not be too acidic. 'If the ink is too acidic it will eat through the parchment,' Brother Luke explained, adding with a sigh that many a fine document had been ruined that way in days gone by. Brother Luke loved his books as if they were his children, Thomas thought.

After Mass and dinner, Thomas and Nicholas worked in the infirmarian's garden. Brother Silvius accompanied them for some of the time, leaving care of the infirmary to his assistant, Brother Dominic. After all the strain of the past days tending Abbot Eidric, the infirmarian seemed to relish this opportunity to be out in the open air, nurturing his plants. He told Thomas that he had still not heard from Matthew Cundulus, but he did not seem unduly disturbed. It was as though he considered the physician's diagnosis an irrelevance, now that the patient was dead.

By the time the bell rang for Vespers, Thomas was ravenous and more than ready for the celebratory meal that Brother Gregory had promised. Usually supper was no more than leftovers from lunch, but this evening the monks were to enjoy a veritable feast. Generals – the plain, ordinary dishes of cereal and vegetables that were the monks' staple fare – were supplemented by pittances – delicious dishes of eggs and fish, including the salmon and pike that Brother Alban had mentioned. To Thomas's joy it was prepared as at home with cinnamon and ginger. To drink, in place of the normal watery ale, there was wine from the abbey's well-stocked cellar.

At the abbot's table, a place had been set for Abbot Eidric, as it would be for every meal for a whole year as a mark of respect and remembrance. The food served up would be given as alms to some poor petitioner, of which there were always many outside the abbey gates. Father Gregory said grace and then uncovered his bread – the sign to the other monks that they could begin eating.

While Brother Alban murmured his way flatly through the teachings of St Paul, the other brethren concentrated on their food in silent pleasure, using sign language to communicate any requests, to the gentle accompaniment of knives scraping lightly against pewter plates and cups tapping on the wooden tables. For Thomas, it was a far cry from the exuberant feasts at home, when his parents and their invited guests gossiped and guffawed, while musicians played, dogs yelped and barked, servants bustled . . . But he enjoyed this feast as much as any, perhaps because he was really hungry, but also because, for the first time since he had arrived at Maundle, he felt truly part of a family.

This sense of well-being continued through Compline, the last service of the day and the one Thomas loved best. Suffused with the glow of candles and twilight gleaming in at the tall perpendicular window behind the altar, the abbey church seemed to Thomas to be a beautiful haven of faith and tranquillity. The monks offered thanks for the day and asked for strength to keep the Devil at bay during the hours of darkness, praying for a quiet night and a perfect end from their Lord: '*Noctem quietam, et finem perfectum concedat nobis Dominus omnipotens*.' The Latin words had a music to them that was deeply comforting, Thomas found.

It was in this service more than any other that he felt the peace of God flow through him, as sure and soothing as the river that ran beneath the monastery walls. '*Pater noster, qui es in caelis* . . .' he recited, joining his fellow brethren in the Lord's Prayer. Compline saw Brother Bernard's masterful skills as a musician show themselves at their finest. His settings of the Nunc Dimittis and the final hymns to the Virgin Mary created the most melodic music Thomas had ever heard. He longed for the day when he would be able to participate in it fully himself, though he feared that might never be, for he was not blessed with a strong singing voice.

The Rule of Benedict decreed that the period following

Compline should be one of silent contemplation. Some monks went straight to bed; others read or sat in thought. Thomas decided to take a stroll before retiring. He walked quietly through the cloisters in his thin-soled night shoes, passing Brother Luke, the librarian, with his slow, halting gait, and Ambrose, who glanced up at him and grinned. The novice had a knife and a piece of wood in his hand and appeared to be carving something. His curiosity getting the better of him, Thomas was about to ask Ambrose what he was doing when he saw Brother Symeon lurking in the shadows and quickly moved on. He had no wish to receive a beating.

But the silence was soon to be broken. Thomas had just reached the south side of the cloister and had stopped to wash his face in the lavatorium, when the cellarium door rattled open and Brother Ignatius, the porter, appeared. His broad face was red and glistening with perspiration and he was panting heavily like a dog. Seeing Thomas, he stumbled towards him and thrust a rolled-up parchment into his hand

'Take this message to the infirmary, boy,' he ordered. 'Quick, do not tarry. Here is important news from the town.' He paused a moment to catch his breath before continuing in a husky undertone, 'Master Cundulus, the physician, is murdered.'

CHAPTER 12

Dear Mother,

I hope this letter finds you well. We are not usually allowed to send letters, but my novice master, Brother Martin, has granted me special permission, with the consent of our new abbot, Father Gregory. He suggested that I write to you to allay any worries you may have with all the turmoil of recent days.

I know you will have been deeply saddened by the death of our beloved Abbot Eidric, as were we all. The brothers here regarded him as a father and mourn his loss greatly. Our consolation is in the knowledge that he has gone to a better place. If any man deserves salvation, it is he. Brother Martin told me today that he was much respected by King Henry, for though born a Yorkist, Father Eidric was never a supporter of King Richard, whom he considered to be a usurper and murderer. I do not think Father would agree! Soon after King Henry was crowned, he made a royal progress to York and stayed at our abbey as the abbot's guest (I wish I had been here then!). Brother Martin fears that with the abbot's death we may lose our royal patronage and struggle to survive. Running the monastery and its grounds is expensive and we do not have great funds. Brother Martin says that King Henry will have little money to spare now in any case, with the expenses of paying his army and the magnificent new palace that he is building near London.

We were all very shocked to hear of the murder of the eminent physician, Matthew Cundulus. I am sure you will have heard of it too. They say he was stabbed to death, Mother, and his heart and tongue cut out. Who would do such a terrible thing? He visited our abbey only days ago to tend to Abbot Eidric and I acted as his guide, showing him around the gardens. I helped him collect plant specimens, which he took away for testing. I liked Master Cundulus, Mother. He was so full of life and so full of knowledge and wisdom. Brother Silvius says that Matthew Cundulus was a very fine physician and his death is a great loss to the world. His murder was a terrible, terrible thing, but it seems that the world is full of terrible things just now. My friend Nicholas says that a monk at Larksby Abbey (Nicholas joined us from there a week ago after it was destroyed by fire) told him that King Richard's bones were unearthed from his grave and thrown to the dogs, and his coffin used as a horse trough!

Not a day goes by that I do not miss you, Mother, and I think of you often. I do not find this an easy life,

but it is not as harsh or arduous as I had feare
is my home now, I know, these brothers my holy fa
and I shall do my best to serve God and make you proud. Do not worry about me. Brother Martin is the best and kindest master any novice could wish to have. He is like a father to me. (I hope that one day he will be abbot.)

St Benedict's Rule forbids us to have personal possessions, as you know, but there are times when I wish I had my animal skulls with me. They always brought me such comfort. I do not suppose anyone wants them now. Please bury them in the garden beneath the oak tree as I had intended.

Give my regards to Father and to Giles. I hope his apprenticeship is progressing well. I say a prayer for you all every night.

Your loving son,

Thomas

* * *

vas no grave, no headstone, just a brown plastic urn nich Mum's last remains were collected. It was like a nt coffee jar – it even had a screw-top lid, as if you might want to unscrew it now and then and take out a spoon of ashes to make a hot drink: instant death. It was probably the cheapest urn you could buy. It wasn't that Dad was mean; he just didn't know what to do with the ashes. He wouldn't bury them and he couldn't just throw them away, so hence the urn. It was just a temporary measure, he said, while he thought about what to do. He didn't want anything fancy, because that would be as bad as having a headstone. I'd have been happy having a headstone, but Dad wouldn't hear of it. Death was death, he said. There was nothing else. He thought graves and headstones were just morbid superstition.

I held the urn, hugged it to my chest, all the way home in the car, as though it was Mum herself, not a piece of unfeeling plastic. Dad didn't really know what to do with the thing, so I took it up to my room and put it on the shelf over the fireplace. I put it right in the centre, and then I put some of Mum's stuff around it – an emerald bracelet she often wore, a piece of sparkly quartz I'd brought her back from a school trip, a dish of white rose petals . . . It made me feel like she was still around the place, still alive some-

how – her spirit anyway. Dad didn't approve – he said it was like a shrine, which it was, I guess, but I didn't see anything wrong in that. I loved Mum, adored her – a shrine was the least she deserved from me. It was the only way I could hold onto her, because Dad wouldn't talk about her. The moment we got back from the cremation he went back to work as if nothing had happened and he never mentioned Mum. It was like she'd never existed. 'We have to move on, Liam,' was all he said. But I didn't want to move on. I wanted to go back – back to that short but tantalizingly untouchable time when Mum had been alive. I wanted my mum back. Was that really so strange?

Chapter 13

In the weeks following the death of Abbot Eidric, life at Maundle Abbey settled once more into a largely tranquil regime of services, study and labour. Father Gregory's rule was not as severe as some – Thomas included – had feared. Indeed, when not in church, the new abbot was rarely to be seen about the abbey, spending his time within the walls of the abbot's lodgings, often in consultation with his closest associates, Brother Alban and Brother Symeon.

Abbot Eidric's plans for the presbytery were set in motion – with one significant alteration: the hand of St Geronimus was no longer to be buried beneath the new altar; instead it was to be displayed in the magnificent reliquary from Larksby Abbey. This news was of particular delight to Brother Symeon, as was evident in his smugly pious smile when it was announced in chapter. He was to be in charge of the relic's display and protection, of pilgrims' access to it and collecting their monetary donations. This was of such importance that a special watching loft was to be built so that the sacristan could keep an eye on the abbey's treasures. In this time of financial straits, the revenue from these relics would be of vital significance to the abbey's future, Father Gregory asseverated. He went on to explain that as well as paying to view the relics, pilgrims would donate money in exchange for indulgences, prayers said on their behalf by the monks to assist their passage into Heaven. This seemed to Thomas a strange idea. Could you really buy your way into Heaven? Surely that went against everything that Jesus had preached.

Financial matters were at the heart of many of the new abbot's homilies. Where Abbot Eidric's recurring theme had been the necessity for spiritual purity, Father Gregory's principal concern, it seemed to Thomas, was for economic prudence. He spoke of the need for good housekeeping, well-kept and regulated stores, carefully managed resources and the restriction of outside labour. He also had a very equivocal attitude towards alms.

Alms were an important element of any monastery's life. It was enshrined in the Rule of St Benedict that monasteries should help the needy. As almoner, Brother Martin was the monk responsible for dispensing these gifts and was less than happy when his new superior suggested that he was being over-generous.

'The king may be able to afford to double his alms to two pennies, but he only pays out money on royal anniversaries. For us it is a constant burden,' the abbot grumbled one day in chapter. 'We cannot afford such largesse.'

'It is our duty to give to the poor,' Brother Martin reminded his superior, 'especially in these times when plagues and wars have caused so much suffering and hardship.'

'I am well aware of our duty, Brother,' Father Gregory remarked sharply. At this point Brother Alban intervened with a suggestion – adopted with enthusiasm by the abbot – that except on special occasions such as the feast of St Geronimus, alms should be given, not in money, but in food and drink.

'He will set the people against us,' Brother Martin complained to Brother Luke in the parlour later, while Thomas and Nicholas sat waiting for their instructions for the day. 'Lord knows we are hardly popular now. Only yesterday I heard a townsman liken us to carrion crows.'

'But nor are we wealthy, Brother,' the librarian argued. 'I think Brother Alban's suggestion has merit. Our Rule calls us to dispense charity; it does not dictate how we are to do it.'

But Brother Martin was not convinced. 'It is all very well for Brother Alban. He is not the one responsible for distributing alms.'

'We each have our cross to bear,' Brother Luke sighed. Then he smiled. 'Mine is teaching young Nicholas here to copy in a clear hand.'

'I d-do my best, Father,' Nicholas stammered apologetically.

'I know you do, my boy,' said Brother Luke. 'And no one can ask more than that.'

Brother Bernard, however, was not so tolerant.

'You do not try hard enough,' he berated Thomas and Nicholas that afternoon when he was teaching them chanting. Brother Bernard liked to give his lessons in the church rather than in the novices' own room because the acoustics of the high vaulted space were, he maintained, so much better. Here, more than anywhere else, the human voice could reach sublimity. 'Singing is a divine gift,' he said. 'Through song we are lifted from the earthly shadows to the kingdom of Heaven.' He looked at the boys with his characteristic blend of vagueness and melancholy and ran his hand over his wispy grey hair. 'Do you not wish to be transported?'

'Yes, Father,' Thomas and Nicholas declared as one. But neither of them found singing easy. To Thomas a tune was as slippery as an eel. One minute it seemed as if he had hold of it, and then the next it had wriggled away and left him. He wondered if he would ever be able to sing like the other brothers. For the present, in church, he followed the advice that the precentor of Larksby Abbey had given Nicholas – 'The worst sin is to be loud and off key. If you cannot sing properly, at least be quiet and unobtrusive.'

Fortunately for Thomas and Nicholas, they were not the only novices with Brother Bernard that afternoon. Ambrose too was there and he had a fine voice. Older than the other two, he had a clear mellifluous tone with none of their adolescent waverings. His singing brought a rare smile to the precentor's face.

'You sing like a seraph,' he enthused. 'Listening to you is like seeing God smile.' Ambrose grinned broadly. The precentor's own smile slipped regretfully. 'If only your companions could halfway match you . . .'

'You praise very highly, Brother.' Standing beneath the archway that led to the sacristy, Brother Symeon cast a dark shadow across the chequered stone floor of the small chapel in the south transept where Brother Bernard and his pupils were gathered. He was wearing his alb, and the white full-length tunic coupled with the unnatural pallor of his skin gave him the appearance of a phantom in the murky light. This sinister impression was intensified by the large round black stone he was holding. In his hands, Thomas thought, the smoothing stone had a sinister quality – it looked more like a weapon than a harmless tool for removing the wrinkles from the church linen. 'Perhaps too highly,' the sacristan added coldly. 'It is God's grace that should be praised for granting Brother Ambrose his gift, not Brother Ambrose himself.'

'Brother, I do not presume to teach you your business, and nor should you presume to teach me mine,' Brother Bernard responded with frost in his melancholy sing-song voice. 'We each serve the Lord in our own way. I have heard similar thoughts to those I express in the mouth of our beloved former abbot, Eidric.' He crossed himself. 'May his soul rest in eternal peace.'

'My concern is only for your pupil, Brother,' said the sacristan in a voice that, to Thomas at least, betrayed not the slightest hint of concern. 'Brother Ambrose may fall in love with his own talent and lose sight of the one from whom it comes. And that surely would be pride, and pride is a mortal sin.' He raised the smoothing stone slightly, an insidious smile creasing his pallid skin. 'Brother Ambrose has already been punished severely for one mortal sin. I am certain he has no wish for further chastisement.'

These words had an immediate and shocking impact on Ambrose. Where but moments before he had been grinning like a fool, now his face began to twitch and contort like a madman's. His breathing became wild and his simple eyes bulged with panic and distress.

'You shall not beat me. You shall not!' he gasped, his lips wet with spittle. 'You shall not!' He sank to his knees, clasping his hands to his face, covering his eyes.

Thomas and Nicholas shrank back, not knowing what to do. But Brother Bernard moved with unusual swiftness, stepping forward and taking hold of Ambrose by the shoulders to quell his shaking. 'I suggest you return to your vestments, Brother,' he said curtly to the sacristan, who turned and departed. He moved so swiftly and silently in his ground-length robe that he seemed more like a spectre than ever, Thomas thought.

It took Brother Bernard some time to calm Ambrose. Then he instructed Thomas and Nicholas to escort their fellow novice to the infirmary. There Brother Silvius administered an infusion of yarrow and honey as a mild sedative and made Brother Ambrose lie down on a bed to rest. He was still trembling, but his agitated muttering had ceased and he seemed a good deal more peaceful.

That night, Ambrose disappeared.

Chapter 14

Thomas was the first to notice Ambrose's absence. Each of the brothers had his own place in the choir stalls, arranged by length of service – the longest-serving monks sitting nearest the abbot. Thomas's place was at the far end of the stalls, away from the altar, between Nicholas and Ambrose. At Matins that morning, Ambrose's place was empty.

Thomas wasn't greatly concerned. Ambrose had recovered sufficiently to attend Compline the previous night, but he had been so badly affected by the sacristan's veiled threat that afternoon that Thomas would not have been surprised if he was back in the infirmary. Besides, it wasn't that unusual for monks to miss Matins through over-sleeping or a protracted visit to the reredorter. Under Abbot Eidric, regular checks had been made, but these had lapsed in the new abbot's reign. Father Gregory had more important matters on his mind, it seemed, than his flock's adherence to their daily rituals.

Ambrose wasn't in the infirmary, however – and nor was he in the dormitory or the reredorter. His bedclothes were ranged untidily, the blanket rucked half on the mattress, half on the floor rushes, as if its owner had got up in haste. Thomas lifted the blanket to put it back on the bed, and in doing so disturbed something that flicked out and thudded against the stone wall. It was the wood carving that he had seen Ambrose working on the night they had received the news of Matthew Cundulus's murder. Thomas bent down and picked it up. It was a figure of some kind, like a little human, carved crudely but not without skill. In general it was well proportioned, but with one odd feature – it had a woman's breasts, but a man's genitals. Thomas wondered what the significance of the figure was – if indeed it had any. Perhaps it was a source of comfort for Ambrose, just as his animal skulls had been for Thomas.

Thomas didn't report Ambrose's absence at once because he didn't want to make trouble for his fellow novice. He remembered only too well the beating in the chapter house. But when Ambrose didn't appear for breakfast, Thomas knew that something was amiss. Ambrose loved his food and was always among the first to reach the refectory when the meal-time bell chimed, no matter where in the abbey he was.

After breakfast Thomas spoke to Brother Martin. He told him of the events he had witnessed in the church the previous day and Ambrose's traumatized reaction. Then he showed the novice master Ambrose's carving. Brother Martin frowned.

'What wickedness is this?' he said, the smile gone from his keen blue eyes. 'Ambrose is a fool.' He gazed at the carving with clear distaste and shook his head. 'I thought he had put this shameful heresy behind him.'

Thomas was bemused. He had no idea what his master was referring to. 'I don't understand, Father,' he said.

'It is better you do not,' Brother Martin replied and would say no more. He walked away in a flurry of robe and cowl and took the offending carving with him.

Ambrose did not reappear and no one seemed at all concerned, which Thomas found strange. Even stranger, no one would even speak of him. When Thomas tried, he was quickly silenced. It was as if Ambrose had never been a member of the abbey. Not even Brother Luke, who was usually so loquacious, would speak of him. But it was Brother Bernard's demeanour that Thomas found most strange. After all, just the day before Ambrose's disappearance the precentor had been praising his protégé to the skies, calling his singing divine. Now, when Thomas mentioned his name, Brother Bernard simply looked vague, as if he had no idea who or what Thomas was talking about.

Nicholas had more success, however. Brother Dominic, the snoring assistant of the infirmarian, had taken it upon himself to be Nicholas's unofficial mentor since his arrival at Maundle. He was younger than most of the other monks and less guarded in manner. If he had information about anything – or anyone – he was more than happy to impart it – especially to Nicholas. The day after Ambrose's departure he told Nicholas what he knew about the vanished novice. Nicholas passed on the information to Thomas later, when they were warming themselves before the fire in the novices' room.

'Ambrose was an alchemist's boy,' Nicholas said. 'He assisted him in his experiments, until the alchemist was accused of sorcery by a local tradesman. The alchemist was tried and found guilty. He was sentenced to hang. But on the eve of his execution, he escaped from his prison cell and has not been seen again. Ambrose was found guilty too, but owing to his youth and Abbot Eidric's intervention, he was reprieved.'

'Abbot Eidric saved him?' Thomas asked wonderingly.

'Yes.' Nicholas nodded. 'He offered to take Ambrose into his care, as long as he renounced his wicked doings and entered the monastery as a novice.'

'A small sacrifice to make for having his life,' Thomas remarked, drawing closer to the fire. Although it was almost summer now, the wind had a hard chill to it that seemed to find its way into every room in the monastery – even this room, which was the warmest in the whole abbey, now that the fire in the calefactory was no longer lit.

'But too much apparently,' Nicholas commented. 'He's run away, like his former master.'

'I think Abbot Eidric's death upset him,' said Thomas. 'He seemed, well, strange since.'

'Has he not always been strange? He seemed so to me from the moment I met him.'

Thomas pondered this as he gazed into the flames.

'He was simple,' he said at last. 'But lately he seemed changed.' He told Nicholas about the evening he had seen him carving in the cloisters. 'There was a strange smile on his face, like he was having a joke at everyone else's expense.' He frowned. 'I can't really explain it.'

'Well, perhaps he was doing just that. Brother Dominic says the carving is of a homunculus – a little human, a hermaphrodite, half man, half woman, which alchemists believe they can conjure through their experiments.'

'But surely no one can really believe that. Only God can create life.'

'Alchemists believe it. Maybe Ambrose believes it.' Nicholas's freckly face was flushed in the firelight. 'All you need, apparently, is a bag of bones, skin and hair. Oh, and some horse dung.' Thomas wrinkled his nose in disgust. 'It is a heresy anyway. Ambrose would have been beaten and probably excommunicated. Perhaps that is why he ran away.'

'*If* he ran away,' Thomas mused, the words out almost before he had thought of them.

'What else could have happened?' Nicholas stared at him, his eyes deep and quizzical. Outside, a bell started to clang, summoning the brothers to Compline. Shadows cast by the fire juddered on the stone walls.

'I don't know, Nicholas,' Thomas sighed. 'Something troubles me, that is all. I have never seen anyone as frightened as Ambrose was in the church that day with Brother Symeon. I fear for him.' He pursed his lips and frowned. 'I fear that something bad has befallen him.'

Chapter 15

Father Gregory's decision to put the abbey's precious relics on display was quickly vindicated, for the long summer days brought an increasing number of pilgrims to Maundle – and a concomitant increase in funds. Accommodating these visitors, however, was not without cost – and not all financial. There was, it seemed, a new breed of pilgrim. They came to the monastery not in retreat from their life, but as a kind of holiday. They would pay for the privilege of viewing and touching the abbey's sacred relics, but they expected the best hospitality in return. They treated the guesthouse like an inn and demanded to be well fed and well 'watered'. They wanted wine, not ale, and as much flesh as they could eat. They quarrelled and shouted, and on more than one occasion fights ensued. Once a man was stabbed, fortunately not fatally.

Some of the monks, Brother Martin prominent among them, wanted a return to former times, when the rules of hospitality were far stricter. Father Gregory, however, would not hear of this. Stricter rules would deter pilgrims, he said, and pilgrims – or at least pilgrims' money – were the lifeblood of the monastery. Brother Alban spoke in support of his superior, pointing out that benefactors were few and far between. The rich now favoured the chantry system over monastic patronage. Instead of giving money to monasteries to have their names entered in 'the book of life' when they died, they were giving it to named priests, who would say masses for their departed souls. What Maundle needed was more pilgrims, not fewer, the prior argued. As expected, Brother Symeon agreed. The more pilgrims visited the abbey, the more prominence his beloved relics received – and, by inference, the more important his own standing became.

Thomas sided with Brother Martin. He respected the novice master's integrity and piety to the same degree that he disrespected the prior's apparent obsession with all matters financial. Surely how best to serve and praise God should be the main concern for the monks, not how best to accumulate funds. Nicholas, however, could see both sides of the argument. 'Brother Alban makes a valid point,' he said. 'I do not think that Larksby Abbey could have continued much longer, even without the fire. Abbot William had been troubled by the decrease in funds, and for some time there were barely enough monks there to run the place – I was the only novice to have joined for several years. A brother told me that all over the country monasteries are dispersing or merging. These are difficult times and require prudent measures.'

Thomas was not convinced. 'Yes, these are difficult times, dangerous times even,' he said, echoing Matthew Cundulus's words, 'but surely it's in such adversity that you have to trust in what you believe; put your faith in God, not Mammon.'

Nicholas grinned at this. 'You see everything so black and white, Thomas,' he said – and they left it at that.

Throughout the summer the relics continued to draw pilgrims from far and wide across the country and from Europe too – including some from Spain, taking advantage of the greater cordiality between the two countries with the betrothal of King Henry's son, Arthur, to the young Spanish princess, Catherine of Aragon. Brother Martin approved of these foreigners, who were more devout and reverential than their English counterparts. Thomas witnessed this himself. He was assisting Brother Symeon with folding the church linen (a task over which the sacristan was most particular) when a party of Spanish pilgrims entered to pay their respects to the abbey's holy relics. They prostrated themselves before the reliquary, murmuring fervent prayers in their own tongue. They were very generous too with their offerings, which, of course, pleased Brother Symeon greatly.

The relics were a great success – so successful indeed that there was talk of enlarging the abbey's collection. But genuine relics were not that easily come by – and important relics were even scarcer. The toenails or strands of hair of obscure saints would not draw crowds as they once might have. Now people wanted bones – preferably entire limbs or a skull – of significant saints; saints who had their own feast days or had notable institutions named after them. And Maundle Abbey, as Thomas inadvertently discovered one night, was about to become the owner of just such a relic.

It was an insufferably hot night with thunder in the air. Thomas woke from another of the strange, intense dreams he had been having for the past months, many of which involved his mother being in danger of some kind. This time, as before, he awoke in a breathless panic, his tunic wet with sweat, bedcover twisted about him. The dormitory was sweltering and airless. For some minutes he lay still in the stifling heat, praying for his panic to subside. He listened for the soothing sound of the water in the river beneath him – but it was a barely audible trickle. They needed rain.

He decided to get up and go to the reredorter. Perhaps the short walk and the act of emptying his bladder would help him settle. He stepped carefully and softly over the rush floor, past the night stairs, which the monks used to enter the church for Matins, beneath the burning night-lights suspended from hooks in the ceiling, all the way to the end of the dormitory. Soundlessly he lifted the latch that opened the reredorter door and slipped through.

He heard the voices at once and froze instinctively. There was no real reason for him to do so – he was entirely within his rights to be here and so were the speakers. But perhaps that was the point: the speaking. No one spoke in the dormitory or the reredorter. It was an abbey rule and one that was taken very seriously, even under the new abbot's laxer regime. But someone was talking – two people – in low, wary voices that suggested they did not wish to be overheard and would not take kindly to being discovered.

He could have pulled the door open and returned to the dormitory but he didn't. Something about the secretiveness of this nocturnal conversation intrigued him, and he stood in silence and listened.

'I can arrange it,' said a low, measured voice, which

Thomas quickly identified as belonging to Brother Alban.

'But a *heart*?' said the second voice, higher in tone, sibilant, and more animated. 'How can you provide a heart? And can you prove its authenticity?' It was Brother Symeon.

'How is not important. It is not your concern. Convincing the world of its authenticity, *that* is your concern.'

'But it might not be that simple. There might be opposition,' the sacristan suggested uncertainly.

'From who? Father Eidric could not stand in our way, and nor shall anyone else.' Brother Alban spoke with such coolness that Thomas felt himself shiver. 'The abbot will be delighted. It's what he has been praying for. Besides, he has other matters on his mind.'

'But a *heart*!' Brother Symeon whined once more.

'In the cathedral of Rouen, inside a lead box, is the heart of King Richard, the Lionheart. No one doubts that is genuine. It has drawn pilgrims for centuries. Famous relics bring wealth and influence – canonization perhaps . . .'

Brother Alban let the words dangle like an enticing jewel. Thomas could almost see the sacristan's small eyes light up at the prospect of spiritual advancement. It was too great a temptation to resist.

'The heart of Saint Geronimus,' he breathed. As if on cue, thunder cracked, presaging a storm.

'No.' Brother Alban's rebuttal was ice itself. 'Greater than that.' He paused an instant as the rain began to fall. 'You shall have the heart of Saint Augustine of Hippo himself.'

One night, about a month after Mum died, I was woken by a noise in my room. I opened my eyes and saw someone over by my shelf. As my eyes found their focus in the gloom, I realized that it was Dad.

'Dad?' I said questioningly. I sat up, suddenly fully awake. 'Dad, what are you doing?'

Dad turned and faced me, looking sort of sheepish. He had the urn in his hands.

'I'm taking this out, Liam,' he said. 'It's not good for you to have it in here like this.'

'What do you mean "not good"?' I queried. 'It's fine. I want it there.' I nodded at the shelf.

'It's stupid, Liam,' Dad said. 'This isn't Mum. She's dead. These are just . . .' He struggled to find the right word, then shrugged. 'They're just ashes.'

'They're Mum's ashes,' I argued. 'And they're all I have.'

Dad shook his head. 'Mum's dead,' he said again.

'Yeah, I know.'

'But you aren't, Liam.' He glanced around my room and threw out a hand. 'This place is like a tomb. You have to get back into your life.'

I had spent a lot of time in my room since Mum died, it was true – in between appointments with counsellors and shrinks and so on. I hadn't been back to school. I hadn't done any of the stuff I used to do, like playing football. I hadn't wanted to see my friends.

'This is my life,' I insisted. 'Now, put the urn back please.'

'You can't bring Mum back to life, Liam. No one can.'

I got out of bed. 'Put the urn back, Dad.'

'You're being stupid, Liam.' Dad put the urn under one arm. He started to unscrew the top.

'Dad!' I cried. I lunged towards him.

Dad warded me off. He took the lid off the urn and put his hand in. He pulled out a handful of ashes. 'See, Liam. They're just ashes. Not Mum, just lifeless dull ashes.'

I lunged again, trying to grab the urn. I knocked Dad's hand and he spilled the ashes. We both watched in shocked stillness as the ashes, like they were in slow motion, sprinkled down to the ground and spread like a dark stain over the pale carpet. For a moment neither of us moved.

All we could do was stare. Then I snatched the urn from Dad and dropped to my knees. I tried to sweep the fallen ashes back into the urn. But when I'd finished there was still a dark smudge on the carpet and a dark smudge on my hand too. I gazed at it through the wetness of welling eyes, felt the first tears dribble down my cheeks. 'Mum,' I whimpered. 'Mum.'

'Liam,' Dad said softly. He put his hand on my shoulder, but I shook it off.

'Go away,' I hissed. 'Go back to your bones. Leave me alone.'

CHAPTER 16

'Thomas!' A hand grasped and shook him. In the distance a bell tolled. 'Thomas, wake yourself!'

He opened his eyes.

'Thomas, do you not hear the bell? You will be late for Matins!' It was Nicholas.

Thomas yawned, then sat up groggily. 'I was dreaming,' he murmured.

'This is no time for dreaming, Thomas. Come, quickly, before the bell ceases.'

Wearily Thomas threw back his blanket and rose from his bed. He followed Nicholas down the night stairs, through the south transept to the choir. They took their places in the stalls just in time. Moments later, Brother Bernard's chant began the service.

This first service of the day was never an easy one for

Thomas, even in the summertime, but today he found it harder than ever to fix his thoughts on the words of the psalms and responses. His mind was drowsy and confused. Snatches of the conversation he had overheard kept sounding in his head. But was it real? Or had he dreamed it? What did it mean?

He didn't go back to bed after Matins, as many of the monks did. Instead, he walked down to the wooden bridge that crossed the river beside the guesthouse. All was quiet there in the brief interval that separated the going to bed of the carousing pilgrims and the rising of the pious. The dawn was glimmering on the horizon. There was a freshness in the air from the night's storm and the grass was wet and lush. The river rushed and roared, as if eager to get the new day started now that it was full once more.

He could hear birds singing in the trees beyond the abbey walls: the syrupy chirrup of blackbirds, the excited trill of wood warblers, the alto coo of pigeons. The multifariousness of their voices and tones was so different from the uniformity of the monks' plainsong, yet equally beautiful and uplifting – although their chorus was wasted on Thomas this morning. He stood and watched the river crinkle and fold over the rocks, which left fleeting swallow-shaped imprints on the surface of the water as it rushed on. Thomas's thoughts were rushing too.

It had not been a dream – in his wakefulness, he knew that now. But what was the significance of the 'secret' conversation he had heard? And what, if anything, should he do about it? Brother Alban had talked of procuring a heart – and not *any* heart but the heart of one of the most celebrated saints in Christendom: St Augustine of Hippo, whose book of Confessions was one of the most copied sacred texts in the world. Maundle Abbey had its own copy, he knew, for it was one of the texts he had been given to practise his copying skills. To have such a relic would be wondrous indeed. But was it genuine? Something about the cellarer's tone had suggested to him that it might not be and that he didn't really care either. It was purely a business matter.

But what most troubled Thomas was Brother Alban's mention of Father Eidric. What had he meant when he'd said that the late abbot hadn't been able to stand in their way? Thomas recalled the chilling tone in which Brother Alban had spoken, and it made him shiver anew. Matthew Cundulus had suggested that the abbot's death had not been of natural causes. What if that had been the case? What if, incredible as it seemed, Abbot Eidric had been murdered because he stood in the way of Brother Alban's plans? Thomas would never have believed a monk capable of such a deed if he had not heard the prior speaking last night. He had sounded like a man who would do anything to achieve his goals.

As he glanced across the inner courtyard, Thomas's gaze fell upon the oak tree under which Matthew Cundulus had found the Death's Angel mushrooms. Had the physician suspected that they might have something to do with Abbot Eidric's sickness? Thomas decided that he needed to discover more about those mushrooms – and he knew a way of going about it. In the library there were a number of old books on natural history – it was one of Brother Luke's specialist subjects. Next time he had an opportunity he would ask the librarian if he could look through those books. Perhaps there he would find what he needed to know.

'Liam!' the voice drifts down to me like a floating leaf. 'Liam!' A momentary flicker in this darkness that is also light. For an instant I feel myself rouse as if to move towards it but then I sink again.

It's not time. The story is only half done; there are still many pages to fill. I open myself and the pen begins to write again.

CHAPTER 17

It was some days before Thomas had the opportunity to visit the library. He and Nicholas were working in the kitchens that week, and Brother Marius, the kitchener, was a hard task master. There were trenches and pots to wash, vegetables to peel and chop, fish to gut and clean . . . At meal times the two novices waited on the tables, carrying the messes of food from the serving hatch that connected the refectory with the kitchen, then collecting them up again when they were empty. They ate their own food alone after the others had finished and left the dining hall. For Thomas this was the hardest part of the job – handling all those dishes laden with delicious food (Brother Marius was an excellent cook) which made him even hungrier than he already was, but knowing he would have to wait another half-hour before enjoying his portion.

At the end of the week, when their stint in the kitchen was done, Thomas and Nicholas had to wash the feet of all of the brothers, as decreed in Chapter 35 of the Rule of St Benedict. This weekly ritual was in memory of Christ's own washing of the feet of his disciples, but much as he respected its significance, Thomas did not find it at all pleasant. The monks – particularly the older ones – had the ugliest and most misshapen feet that he had ever seen. They were a mess of bunions and calluses, flaking skin and gnarled toes with sharp yellow nails. Many of them smelled bad too in the summer heat, and he had to hold his breath to avoid inhaling the rancid odour. When the last pair of feet had been washed, he and Nicholas breathed a sigh of relief. They made faces of disgust at one another as they emptied out their pails of warm water into the lavatorium.

'I'm glad that is over,' said Nicholas, and Thomas quickly concurred.

They had hardly spoken to one another in days, for as well as being a hard task master, Brother Marius allowed only culinary conversation among his workers, and silence was strictly enforced in the dormitory. Now, at last, the two young monks had some free time on their own and Thomas was able to talk to Nicholas about the conversation he had overheard in the reredorter. Nicholas agreed with Thomas that it sounded suspicious. Neither of them liked or trusted Brother Symeon and both were unsure of Brother Alban.

'He is always so expressionless,' said Nicholas. 'You never know what he is really thinking.'

Thomas told his friend of his plan to research the Death's Angel mushroom in the library.

'But what do we do if you find out that Abbot Eidric was poisoned by mushrooms?' Nicholas pondered.

'We talk to Brother Martin,' said Thomas decisively. 'Tell him everything and let him decide what to do about it.' Nicholas agreed that this was a good plan.

'I'll approach Brother Luke this evening after Vespers,' said Thomas.

Brother Luke was one of the more talkative of the monks, though his talk was almost exclusively about books. He was especially fond of illustrated books, having been a skilful artist himself before failing eyesight had hindered him. He listened with keen interest to Thomas's enquiry about a suitable book on natural history.

'There is a fine plant encyclopaedia in the library, compiled by a monk who lived here once – Brother Dorian,' the librarian enthused, running his hand through his unruly orange hair so that it stood up around his tonsure like a crown. 'You will find few finer examples of the illustrator's art. Brother Dorian was a consummate artist; I only wish I could have met him.' His heavy jowls drooped. 'Alas, our paths failed to cross by nearly two hundred years. Only a blink of an eye in God's time, but an eternity in our own.'

'May I see the book?' Thomas asked.

Brother Luke was only too happy to oblige. 'Why, certainly, my son, certainly,' he said.

The book was kept in an armorium, a locked cupboard in one corner of the library, which contained Brother Luke's most precious treasures, arranged carefully by subject. The librarian ran his finger along the spines of Hildegard's *Medicine*, *The Compendium of Medicine*, and Pliny the Elder's *Historia Naturalis*, before it rested on Brother Dorian's tome. With loving care, he removed the book from its shelf and carried it to one of the lecterns. It was not an easy task, for the book was heavy and the librarian had a marked limp.

'Feast your eyes on the glory of God,' he intoned, a little breathlessly.

With appropriate reverence, Thomas opened *A Natural History of Plants in Britain*. He leafed through the pages, marvelling at the beauty of the pictures and the intricacy of the rubrication, in which capital letters themselves became artful illustrations.

'Alas,' sighed Brother Luke, 'the art of illustration is no longer at the height it once was. Competency has replaced imagination.' With this he limped away to attend to some library business, leaving Thomas alone with Brother Dorian's book.

Thomas worked his way through the book until, at last, he came to the section he had been seeking – fungi. Here were toadstools and mushrooms of all varieties, each meticulously illustrated and with a brief accompanying text. And there it was, the entry he had been looking for: *Amanita bisporigera*, the Death's Angel. His finger trembled a little on the page – his whole hand tingled with nerves – as he studied the picture. It was just as he remembered from the day he had collected one for Matthew Cundulus from under the oak tree: a snow-white mushroom with a delicate veil, fine as an angel's hair, around the stem. But, as its name suggested, it was deadly – one of the most poisonous plants in all the world. The smallest amount could kill a man: 'A man who partaketh of these mushrooms must pray to God for his deliverance,' Thomas read, 'for earthly remedy is there none. Lest God spare him, he must surely die.'

Brother Dorian, it seemed, had observed the fatal effects of the mushroom at first hand, for he described them in detail. It could take half a day before the victim showed symptoms of poisoning, then collapse would be followed by severe stomach cramps, vomiting and diarrhoea. Though he might briefly appear to recover, the victim would soon be afflicted by restlessness and convulsions before losing consciousness. It was then only a matter of time before death took hold. From what Thomas knew of Abbot Eidric's demise, these details were a perfect fit. He wondered if Matthew Cundulus had come to the same conclusion before his brutal murder. And then an uncomfortable thought entered his head: was the timing of the physician's death not a coincidence? Had he been killed because of what he had discovered, and in order to prevent him from revealing it? If that was the case, then what Thomas was doing now could be very dangerous indeed.

Something clattered behind him and made him start. Glancing round, he saw it was only the librarian knocking into one of the wooden writing desks as he limped across the room.

'Did you find what you were looking for?' Brother Luke asked with an enquiring smile.

'I'm not sure,' Thomas replied. He felt suddenly wary. He liked Brother Luke, but he felt vulnerable. He would confide in Brother Martin, he decided, and Brother Martin alone.

CHAPTER 18

At chapter next morning Father Gregory introduced a visitor.

'Brothers, I would like you to join me in welcoming Doctor Stefan Langfell.' He indicated a tall man dressed all in black – black doublet, hose and shoes – with a large silver cross around his neck. He was very thin, which made him seem even taller. He wore no cap, and his dark hair was grey at the temples and neatly cut to his head. He had a small well-trimmed beard and moustache, between which his thin lips were barely visible. His nose was slightly hooked and his eyes deep-set and dark. If you were looking for someone to play Death in a morality play, thought Thomas, then this man would be perfect. Even his smile was sinister – a mere crinkle of the mouth when Father Gregory said his name. Thomas had an odd feeling that he had seen him somewhere before, though he could not think where. 'Doctor Langfell is conducting some important experiments,' the abbot continued, 'and will be residing in the inner gatehouse as my personal guest for an indefinite period. The nature of his work requires the utmost concentration and privacy, and I would instruct that no one visit his lodgings without consulting me first.'

Brother Symeon stood up. 'Might we enquire, Father Abbot,' he wheedled, 'what nature these experiments will take?'

Father Gregory gave the sacristan a cold stare. 'That is not your concern at this time, Brother,' he replied. 'Suffice it to say that these experiments are of the utmost importance.'

'Importance for whom, Father?' Brother Martin dared to ask.

'For mankind, Brother,' the abbot uttered brusquely – and he would say no more.

'That was so mysterious,' said Nicholas while the novices waited in the parlour for Brother Martin.

'It was.' Thomas nodded. He told Nicholas of the strange feeling he had had that he had seen the new visitor before.

'He isn't the sort of man you would forget easily,' Nicholas remarked.

'No,' Thomas agreed, adding, 'even if you wanted to.' Like all the monks, he supposed, he wondered just what the experiments could be that Dr Langfell was conducting and why they were so important. Were these the other matters that Brother Alban had said were on the abbot's mind?

Brother Martin arrived. 'I see you two are deep in discussion,' he said amiably. 'Talking about our mysterious visitor, no doubt.'

The two novices nodded.

'Father Gregory must have his reasons for keeping such secrets,' the novice master commented. 'We must trust they are good ones.' But his look was more doubtful than trusting, Thomas thought. It seemed like a good moment to broach the subject of his findings.

'I have something I wish to confide, Father,' he said.

For the next twenty minutes or so Thomas told the novice master all he knew and suspected about the death of Abbot Eidric. He told him of Matthew Cundulus's visit to the monastery, of his belief that the abbot had died of unnatural causes, and about the Death's Angel mushrooms and his research in the library. Brother Martin listened intently, asking questions now and then.

'I am surprised Brother Silvius did not pass on the doctor's suspicions,' he said when Thomas had finished his narrative.

'Matthew Cundulus asked him not to, until they were confirmed,' Thomas defended the infirmarian. 'And they never were.'

'No,' Brother Martin agreed thoughtfully. He appeared deeply concerned by what Thomas had told him.

Thomas could sense Nicholas's eyes on him, prompting him to reveal the conversation he had overheard in the reredorter. But Thomas hesitated. He wasn't sure it was right to report what he should not have heard. Might it not make him seem like a spy? Brother Martin was evidently aware of his dilemma, for he said softly, 'There is something else troubling you, Thomas. It would be better to tell. Any confidence is safe with me.'

So Thomas told the novice master of the conversation he had overheard.

'The heart of Saint Augustine!' Brother Martin raised his eyebrows. 'That would indeed be a most wondrous relic to possess – and lucrative besides.' He smiled wryly. 'I sense that you are not altogether convinced by this miraculous acquisition.'

'It is not for me to question,' said Thomas humbly.

'Perhaps not. But you do – and I suspect that you are right to do so. These are troubled times.' Brother Martin looked out into the cloister, where the bright sunshine dazzled through the colonnades, casting long blocks of shadow across the stonework. 'A young monk once had a vision while sitting in those cloisters. He was reciting psalms when a bright angelic figure appeared walking towards him, wearing white vestments and a jewelled crown. He explained to the monk that he was the abbey's first abbot, Walter, and that the jewels in his crown represented the souls he had acquired for God during his time as abbot. That young monk went on to become abbot himself and acquire many jewels in his own crown.' He turned his gaze on the two novices. 'I was one of them – for that monk was Father Eidric, and truly he was a father to us all.' His wistful expression became a frown. 'How many jewels, I wonder, will adorn Abbot Gregory's crown?'

Thomas and Nicholas remained silent. It was not a question that required an answer.

Uncle Jack showed up a couple of months after Mum's death. He'd been out of the country for about six months. Most of this time he'd been in Bali in Indonesia, where he'd been working as a driver and guide with a company that ran tours to volcanoes and other sites. The guy who owned the company was a friend of his. Uncle Jack had friends all over the place. He never stayed put anywhere for long. It really annoyed Mum. She said he was just a big boy and it was about time he grew up. 'Feckless' was how she described him. 'He's always waiting for something to turn up,' she said once, 'like it's his right not to have to work for anything.'

Uncle Jack and Dad were like chalk and cheese really. Dad was serious, studious, hard-working, scientific; Jack was happy-go-lucky, flighty, superstitious, a chancer. You'd hardly have thought they could be brothers. But though they were very different, they got on surprisingly well. Dad always took Uncle Jack in when he needed somewhere to stay between trips. In fact he really seemed to like having him around. Which was a source of conflict between him and Mum. Uncle Jack irritated her intensely.

I liked Uncle Jack. He was fun, good-natured and refreshingly light in contrast to my parents. I didn't like the effect he had on Mum, but I looked forward to his visits. And they never lasted long. There was always some new project on the horizon, some new opportunity – a brilliant venture that would make his fortune, though of course it never did, or at least hadn't so far. He was a gambler too, so any money he ever did make soon disappeared. Which was another thing that annoyed Mum.

I always found it easy to talk to Uncle Jack in a way that I didn't with Dad, so I was pleased to see him when he arrived from Bali that day, out of the blue, penniless as usual (he said that rising fuel costs had bankrupted the tour company, but I reckoned it was more likely he'd gambled all the funds away). I guess it helped Dad too because he didn't have to worry about me so much. He could get on with his work and leave me in the not exactly capable but at any rate adult hands of his brother Jack. Just his presence seemed to lift the mood of the house. He was so full of life and laughter and stories. I couldn't imagine him ever being upset or unhappy about anything.

That night he arrived I was at just about my lowest ebb. I was so paralysed by loss and grief, I could barely get out of bed. Yet within a few days he'd somehow managed to achieve what no doctor, counsellor or therapist had: he'd made me smile. He told me stories about climbing to the top of volcanoes where the ground was so hot it melted your shoes. He told me about the tiny village in whose trees, every evening just before dusk, thousands of white herons gathered – the souls, local legend had it, of young lovers killed in a civil war in the 1960s. He told me about the ancient and sacred elephant caves and the festival of Nyepi, on the eve of which people strewed banana skins outside their front doors and banged drums before lapsing into silence for an entire day to confuse the evil spirits.

'I made enough noise, I can tell you, cursing each time

I slipped on one of those damn banana skins,' he laughed. And I laughed too, then stopped, appalled somehow at the strangeness of the sound.

'It's OK, Liam, you're allowed to laugh,' Uncle Jack assured me.

'Am I?' I said. I was frowning now. But I'd crossed a barrier. Uncle Jack had brought me out of Hell. Not very far out, but out – that was the important thing.

CHAPTER 19

Little was seen of the abbey's special guest, but the rumours about his purpose quickly grew. Brother Dominic told Nicholas that Dr Langfell was an eminent astronomer sent by the Pope himself to carry out experiments and research that would refute recent heretical theories about man's place in the universe. Thomas thought this unlikely. He just didn't see the doctor as a 'stargazer' somehow. Another rumour suggested that Dr Langfell was an agent of the Inquisition, which seemed a great deal more plausible to Thomas. The man was certainly menacing enough.

Whatever the doctor's line of work, he seemed to be busy at all hours. If Thomas went for a walk after Matins, there was invariably a light burning in the windows of the inner gatehouse, through which he could see shadows moving. It was all, as Nicholas had remarked, very mysterious.

The building work on the new presbytery was now well under way. The old high altar had been demolished and a temporary altar erected in the monks' choir. The masons had strict instructions from Brother Symeon that they were not to disrupt the daily services, but it was inevitable that they would. When Thomas was helping the sacristan with his duties one day, he heard one of the senior masons complain that it was unreasonable to expect a man clinging to a rope or halfway up a ladder to just suspend what he was doing for half an hour while the monks said their prayers.

'Perhaps you would like to see for yourself, Brother,' the man said gruffly, gesturing at a tall ladder perched against the south wall of the presbytery.

Brother Symeon glanced up along the ladder and went even paler than usual. 'That won't be necessary,' he said with a look of utter terror.

A compromise was reached. The workmen could continue their labours during services, as long as they observed a strict rule of silence. But in practice, this rule was often broken.

At any other time, the intrusion into his church would certainly have been the cause of major upset to Brother Symeon. But at the present moment, with the relics bringing in ever more pilgrims and with the impending unveiling of St Augustine's heart about to take him to new heights of esteem and glory, the sacristan was well pleased with his lot and unusually amenable. He walked around the abbey with a self-satisfied smile that Thomas for one found even less appealing than his former expression of disapproval.

The sacristan's standing had been further enhanced by the recent introduction of incunabulae. It was a common practice, approved by his holiness the Pope, for these printed indulgences to be sold by the Church to guilty Christians, promising absolution from sins. Maundle's incunabulae were small scrolls of parchment, produced by Brother Luke and his scribes (Thomas among them), featuring three illuminated characters side by side with a text offering absolution. They had proved very popular with pilgrims, who were willing to pay handsomely for them. Others, however, were far less enthusiastic – Brother Luke, for example, who complained that producing the incunabulae was diverting his scribes from the more important task of copying sacred texts. But his grumbles fell on deaf ears. The demand for incunabulae only increased.

Thomas himself was disappointed that in the days and then weeks that followed his conversation with Brother

Martin, nothing seemed to result. The acquiring of St Augustine's heart had gone ahead and, though it had not had official verification, the organ's authenticity was not openly disputed. The desire to believe, it seemed, outweighed any other impulse. Not that Thomas wished the relic to be declared false. To have a relic of such deep holiness, if it were genuine, would indeed be wondrous and add greatly to the sanctity of the church. But surely proof was needed that it was genuine. Of course, Thomas had no way of knowing what had been said among the obedientiaries or if indeed they had even met to discuss the matter, but he would like to have known that some challenge had been made. And what about the matter of Abbot Eidric's death? Had his findings not warranted some kind of inquiry? It seemed not. He knew that Brother Martin had not kept what he had been told to himself, for one afternoon Brother Silvius talked to Thomas on the matter.

Thomas was in the infirmary, assisting the infirmarian with the task of blood-letting. Losing blood in this way was believed to improve general physical and spiritual health, cleansing mind and body of unhealthy desires. A cut was made in the vein of the arm and the blood allowed to flow into a bowl. Thomas had yet to experience the process, but his time would come, for every monk in the community underwent blood-letting at least once a year. The majority welcomed it too, for they were excused from all duties in the days it took to regain their strength – and were even allowed to eat meat to aid their recovery. On this particular day it was Brother Dominic who was being let – which is why Brother Silvius needed outside assistance.

'Brother Martin told me that you revealed Matthew Cundulus's suspicions to him,' the infirmarian remarked suddenly as he watched the blood dripping from his assistant's arm.

'Yes,' Thomas replied, a little taken aback.

'I wonder if that was wise.'

'To talk to Brother Martin?'

'No. To open a closed wound.'

'I would not have done so, Father, had it not been for the discoveries I made about the Death's Angel mushroom.'

'Ah, yes, the deadly fungi.' Brother Silvius removed the blood-filled bowl and replaced it with another. 'You did very well there, my son. I think you might make an excellent infirmarian yourself one day. You have a fine inquisitive mind.'

'Thank you, Father.'

'But a mind can be *too* inquisitive, Thomas. Sometimes it is better to go for the easy answer.'

'Even if it is wrong?' Thomas spoke without thinking.

Brother Silvius gave a world-weary smile. 'Who is to say it *is* wrong? Abbot Eidric may have died of mushroom poisoning or sweating sickness or some other cause. And even if he did die as a result of these deadly mushrooms, there is no evidence that any malice was involved. There are many plants – hemlock, wolf's bane – which will kill if taken in large doses, but in small amounts may aid a patient's recovery. Accidents have been known to happen. Whatever the case, we shall never know. The abbot is dead and with his maker. God rest his soul.' He crossed himself and, turning his hale face towards Thomas, looked him straight in the eyes. 'The rest of us must live on in this place.'

To Thomas, it felt like a warning. But about what exactly? Not taking his investigations any further for the good of the monastery – or for his own safety? Or was there something else behind the infirmarian's words? He didn't know, but he certainly wasn't reassured.

He slept badly again that night. When he opened his eyes, the night was still darkening. Through the window he could see the stars glistening in the unclouded sky and the moon watching over them like a mother. How he missed *his* mother. If he'd been at home now, she would have soothed him to sleep with her soft hands and gentle voice.

But he wasn't at home and he didn't know whether he would ever see his mother again. That thought made him feel so melancholy his eyes moistened and he had to bite his lip to keep back the tears. Lying here would do no good, he decided. Quietly he got up and put on his scapula over his tunic. He crept through the sleeping dormitory and down the day stairs that led out into the cloisters. He could hear carousing still from the main guesthouse, where some of the less pious pilgrims were burning the night oil. Thinking he would sit a while by the river, he walked out into the inner courtyard. But something stopped him in his tracks.

Ahead of him, pacing towards the lit-up inner gatehouse was Abbot Gregory. But it wasn't the sight of the abbot that made Thomas freeze in shocked surprise, it was the identity of the man hurrying behind him. Even in the charcoal gloom there was no mistaking his distinctive, impatient stride. It was Thomas's father.

It's always worst at night, lying awake in the dark thinking about Mum, recalling good memories like Christmas or birthdays or holidays we've been on. When I was about eight or nine we went to the south of France for a week. Before we left, Mum bought me this foam football, and everywhere we went on holiday I took it with me. We visited some ancient underground caves that were really cool – in every sense. I wasn't allowed to take my ball in though. I remember these amazing stalactites (I know they were called stalactites rather than stalagmites because Dad said this thing about tights falling down). They were huge and really impressive. That trip was Dad's idea of heaven. He was really into geology and stuff; Mum wasn't. The bit she liked best was when some musicians started playing in a candlelit boat on an underground lake. They just floated in out of the darkness. It was kind of eerie, but cool too. I expect Dad thought it a bit gimmicky. He was sniffy about anything touristy – which is why my other memory of that holiday is kind of surprising: we went on a day trip to this holy healing place called Lourdes. That must have been Mum's idea. She wasn't really religious, but she'd been brought up as a Catholic and she liked visiting churches and stuff.

My memories of our trip to Lourdes are sketchy. They are made up of a random collection of snapshots rather than a continuous video. I remember Mum reading me stuff from a book about the history of Lourdes and a girl called Bernadette, who claimed to have seen the Virgin Mary there several times. After that, the grotto where she had these 'apparitions' and the water that ran there was supposed to have miraculous properties. Lots of sick and disabled people went there on pilgrimages to get cured. I have this really vivid memory of people on crutches and in wheelchairs going up a long, long drive towards the church, built over the grotto. I was kicking my foam football, of course, and they were getting in my way.

I remember too going into the church with Mum and then down to the grotto. Dad didn't come on that bit. He was in a bit of a grump by then, I recall, and went off to sit down by the river. I don't remember what the grotto was like but I do remember all these candles, rows and rows of them, many with little notes attached with names of people to pray for. Mum bought three candles, one for each of us, and she let me light one and place it in the rack. Then she put her arm around me and pulled me tight and we stood for a few minutes just staring at all those wavering candle flames. 'Tiny flickers of hope', Mum called them, but when I hear her say it now in my head, her voice sounds sad rather than hopeful.

There were lots of shops and stalls around Lourdes selling souvenirs – statues and medallions, rosaries and crucifixes, Bibles and certificates, and bottles of holy water. I wanted to buy one of these. I made a bit of a fuss, I recall, because Dad was really against it. He said the whole thing was superstitious nonsense and a tourist rip-off. Mum said he was just being grumpy. She said that I should have a memento of the place if I wanted it. So she let me choose one: a little glass bottle – like a perfume bottle really – with a round silver top and a small, thin silver medallion attached to it halfway down with a scene of Bernadette kneeling in front of the Virgin Mary.

I've still got it on my shelf. I look at it often, willing it to perform a miracle. I know Mum's dead and nothing can bring her back to life. But if only I could see her again – have an apparition of her, like Bernadette with the Virgin Mary. If I could just see her one last time and tell her I love her.

CHAPTER 20

The days that followed were difficult for Thomas. He was distracted and found it hard to concentrate in the daily services and on the tasks he was given. Brother Bernard reprimanded him a number of times for his lack of attention in church, and he made so many mistakes in his copying that even the usually genial Brother Luke was moved to censure him. 'I might expect such errors of Nicholas,' he said, 'but not of you, Thomas. Brother Dorian would not be impressed.'

'I'm sorry, Father,' Thomas apologized – and he really was. But his fingers and his mind were not on the same plane.

There were so many things that he did not understand. It was as if everything that was happening around him in the abbey and at home (no, at his former home, his parents' house; *this* was his home now) was a mystery. It seemed all to be connected, but he did not know how. Perplexed and confused at seeing his father with the abbot, he had spoken with Brother Martin the following morning after chapter. The novice master was intrigued but could offer no explanation. 'Father Gregory keeps his own counsel,' he said. 'It seems there are matters he does not wish to share even with his obedientiaries.' He frowned, two grooves framing the pockmark between his eyebrows to form a rough letter A. 'Well, not with this obedientiary at any rate. I believe that Brother Alban has his confidence – and Brother Symeon too, but that is all.'

Thomas did not dare speak to the abbot and he was wary of approaching Brother Alban and Symeon too since the conversation he had overheard. He remained confused despite his many prayers for enlightenment and guidance. Why would his father visit the abbey on business in the middle of the night? Even if he did not wish to leave the goldsmith's shop during the day, why wait until so late to make his call? It was not like his father. 'Early to rise, early to bed' was his unwavering regime. Thomas had seen him on the way to the inner gatehouse, so was he involved in some way with Dr Langfell's mysterious experiments? But what part could he play? He wasn't what you would call a spiritual man. He was a wealthy and influential businessman, a goldsmith. But what use was a goldsmith to Father Gregory and Dr Langfell? The more Thomas thought about it all, the more muddled it all appeared to be.

Amongst his confusion was a sense of hurt too: that having come to the monastery, his father had not sought him out. It was months, after all, since they had last seen one another, and though their relationship was not the closest, they were still father and son. Did Thomas mean so little to his father? And now something new was troubling him. He recalled where he had first seen Dr Langfell. It had been at home some years before. Thomas had only glimpsed the man briefly through the doorway of his father's study before the door was shut firmly, but the dark, sinister face had left a powerful impression. So his father had known Dr Langfell even before the other night.

Thomas's turmoil was soon to deepen further. A new and shocking misfortune befell the abbey: before Matins early one morning, Brother Symeon was found dead on the flagstones in front of the altar. There were no witnesses to what had occurred, but it appeared that the sacristan had fallen from a high ladder in the presbytery. His skull was smashed and his neck broken, his white alb wrapped about his limp body like a bloody shroud. Brother Martin discovered him and quickly summoned the infirmarian, but he was beyond saving. The fall had killed him.

It was a mystery why Brother Symeon had climbed the ladder. The explanation expressed in chapter was that the sacristan had wished to experience in advance the view he would have of his precious relics when his new platform was built. In private, however, opinions were more critical. Brother Symeon was not a popular member of the community and the general feeling seemed to be that his attitude of spiritual superiority had caused his downfall – or 'pride comes before a fall', as Nicholas had put it. 'He cared far more for those relics than for any of his fellow brethren,' he said to Thomas when they sat in the novices' room the day after Brother Symeon's funeral.

'I know.' Thomas nodded. 'I didn't like him either – especially after that business with Ambrose. But I wouldn't have wished him dead.'

'No,' Nicholas agreed. For a while the two fell into silent thought.

Thomas stared at the white stripes of sunlight that patterned the stone floor. He considered Brother Symeon's funeral. It had not had any of the emotional power of Abbot Eidric's. It was not unnatural that the death of an abbot – especially one as esteemed as Father Eidric – would be treated as a more major event than the passing of one of the brethren – even as senior an obedientiary as Brother Symeon. But there was more to it than that. The manner in which Father Gregory had conducted the service had been altogether different from Abbot Eidric's. He had seemed distracted, uninvolved, more aloof than ever, his words almost garbled, as if he wanted the whole thing over as quickly as possible so that he could get back to more pressing matters. He was a man with important affairs on his mind, and they didn't, it appeared, concern Brother Symeon, even though he had been one of the abbot's closest associates in the abbey.

Once more Thomas's thoughts returned to that night when he had seen his father following Father Gregory across the courtyard to the gatehouse occupied by Dr Stefan Langfell. Thomas was sure that it was the activity in that place that was the focus of the abbot's attention. But what was going on there? And how was his father involved? These questions continued to irk him. But now something new was concerning him.

'Nicholas?' he said questioningly.

'Yes, Thomas,' his friend replied. 'Something is worrying you, I can see. You've been frowning at the floor as though it were some complex mathematical problem.'

'Have I?' Thomas said. He touched one hand to his brow and felt the deep grooves there. It was odd, he thought in passing, how serious he had become since joining the abbey. There seemed to be little trace now of the carefree boy he had been, who used to ride and hawk and play skittles with his friends. 'There is something – something that doesn't seem right.' He looked into Nicholas's pale, freckly, candid face and wished for an instant that everything could be so straightforward. 'It's about Brother Symeon.'

'What of Brother Symeon?'

As one, the two novices turned their heads towards the doorway through which Brother Martin had just appeared. He walked towards them, rephrasing his question. 'Does something trouble you about Brother Symeon, Thomas?' he enquired.

'Yes, Father.' Thomas nodded.

Adjusting his scapula, the novice master sat down next to him on the stone bench. 'Tell me,' he said simply.

Thomas frowned once more. 'Brother Symeon was afraid of heights,' he said.

Brother Martin smiled quizzically. 'How could you possibly know that?' he asked, his blue eyes bright with a mixture of surprise and amusement.

'A little while ago, when I was helping him, one of the masons challenged him to climb a ladder.' Thomas's frown intensified. 'I have never seen anyone so terrified.'

'I see,' said Brother Martin. He looked thoughtful. 'You are puzzled as to how he could have climbed the ladder that ultimately caused his death.'

Thomas nodded again. 'I couldn't have done it, if I'd had such a fear.'

'No,' Brother Martin concurred. 'But you are not Brother Symeon, Thomas – and I thank God for that.' This apparent criticism of the recently deceased sacristan drew questioning stares from both Thomas and Nicholas.

'Brother Symeon believed himself to be closer to the Almighty than the rest of us,' Brother Martin continued. 'Who can say what he would not have done to confirm this belief?'

The questioning stares deepened.

'The truth is that none of us knows,' Brother Martin concluded. 'All we can do is pray for his soul.'

This remark pained Thomas, for it reminded him of his duty – a duty he had neglected. In all his pondering and puzzling, he had forgotten to pray for his dead brother.

Brother Martin smiled broadly. 'Thomas, oh, Thomas,' he laughed. 'I am sure that one day you shall be abbot. Already you carry all the troubles of this place on your shoulders.'

Nicholas laughed too at the aptness of the novice master's words. For his part, Thomas just sighed. Never mind being abbot, the day when he would take his final vows still seemed a long way off. There was yet so much for him to learn and comprehend. Would he ever be as wise and knowledgeable as Brother Martin? At this moment the idea seemed quite inconceivable.

I was the one who was accident-prone. Mum used to joke about it in that weary, slightly sad manner she had. (That's the expression on her face in my favourite picture of her. It's a photo of the two of us when I was about three years old, I guess. I'm leaning my blond head against her arm with a big-eyed earnest look, and she towers over me, her long light-brown hair almost touching my ear. She's smiling, but a little tentatively, like she's afraid something terrible might happen at any moment – which, given my record, isn't surprising, I suppose.) I've lost count of all the times I've been to Casualty. As a toddler, just walking, I fell over and hit my head on the concrete floor in the kitchen. Mum was worried I had concussion and took me up to hospital. A little while later I tripped over in the garden and cut my head open on a sharp stone. I went to hospital again but the blood had made it look worse than it actually was.

In the years that followed, I fell off my bike and out of

a tree – breaking my wrist and collarbone respectively. On numerous occasions Mum had been summoned by nursery or school because I'd had some mishap. And, of course, when I got into playing football, it was inevitable that I'd end up injured. I had an x-ray on a swollen ankle that luckily turned out not to be broken. I had suspected concussion for a second time when I banged my head against a goalpost. Only a few months ago I'd had to have stitches in my leg after being studded in a tackle. Each time it was Mum who took me to the hospital and waited with me and talked to the nurses and doctors and sorted everything out for her walking accident of a son. I'd escaped all those accidents, like a cat with nine lives, but the last and cruellest laugh had been on me, because an accident, a catastrophic, inescapable accident, had ambushed my lovely un-accident-prone Mum. And no one had been there to save her.

CHAPTER 21

Summer was drawing to a close. The cloisters were no longer a sun trap where the monks could sit and read in light and warmth even in the early evening. By the end of the early evening service of Vespers the days were dusky, and the dark fell quickly after.

Thomas tried hard to put aside his concerns and confusions and concentrate on his duties. He spent more and more time in the library, developing his copying and illustrating skills under the critical yet increasingly appreciative eye of Brother Luke, who had identified a rare gift in the young novice and was determined to enhance it. 'A skill like yours must not be allowed to go to waste,' he insisted. 'It would be a crime against God. Let others tend the gardens or the sick – your place is here, in the library, adorning the sacred texts which are the spiritual food of our order.'

Thomas was happy to spend so much time in the library. He liked Brother Luke and shared the librarian's fondness for books, an enthusiasm he had inherited from his mother. She had often read to him when he was young. Her favourite book was *The Mirror of the Blessed Life of Jesus Christ*, a devotional work written originally in Latin and translated into English by a monk. The book actually belonged to Thomas's father, having been given to him by the printer William Caxton in appreciation of some service rendered, but the goldsmith had little interest in books beyond business ledgers. Thomas had loved hearing his mother read from the book, but it was the woodcut illustrations that had most appealed to him. They had a simplicity and elegance that seemed to him to be the perfect accompaniment to the story.

It was to Thomas's surprise and pleasure that he found a copy of the book in the abbey library one late August afternoon. He took it down from the shelf and held it open on the desk before him, admiring anew the illustration of the Nativity, his eyes drawn as ever to the haloed figure of Mary, hands clasped in prayer, gazing down in adoration at the tiny baby in the crib, one hand reaching up to her. He'd always found it a very uplifting picture in the past and yet, staring at it today, he felt suddenly overwhelmed by a sense of melancholy. It was something about the poses of mother and child: the lack of touch, the gap between them, their 'apartness', the mortal mother and her divine son. But it was more than that. Looking at the illustration, Thomas was reminded of his separation from his own mother – of how deep and unending that separation must be, at least in this life. Before he knew it, there were tears in his eyes and he had to wipe them away quickly to prevent them dripping onto the page in front of him.

Sighing, he shut the book and returned to his writing desk and the task Brother Luke had set him: illustrating a homily by Father Eidric on the life of Our Lady. For the remainder of the afternoon, before the bell rang for Vespers, he worked assiduously with quill pen and inks, creating a historiated initial – a letter O with a picture of Mary within – to begin the homily. He thought he was working to take his mind off his distress, but when Brother Luke came by and admired his handiwork, Thomas realized that what he had in fact produced was a portrait of his own mother. It was, he was quite certain, the finest piece of illustration he had done so far, and yet it afforded him little contentment.

His mind was further troubled by the news that Nicholas revealed later. Apart from in services and at meal times, the two had barely spent any time in each other's company for some days – for as Thomas had been occupied in the library, so Nicholas had been busy assisting Brother Silvius and Brother Dominic in the infirmary. This evening, as they exited the church and entered the cloister after Vespers, Nicholas tugged at Thomas's robe and gestured with his head for his friend to follow him.

'What is it, Nicholas?' Thomas asked when they were alone in the novices' room. Nicholas opened his mouth to speak, then closed it again, an anxious look in his deep-set eyes. He turned and went over to the door. Lifting the latch, he opened it and peered out into the cloister, before pulling the heavy wooden door shut again.

'Whatever's the matter?' Thomas enquired, both intrigued and concerned by his fellow novice's furtive behaviour.

Nicholas sighed, a heavy frown creasing his freckly forehead. 'I just wanted to be sure we wouldn't be disturbed,' he said. 'Or overheard,' he added mysteriously – and when he'd finished speaking, Thomas understood why that should be.

Earlier that day, Brother Silvius had sent Nicholas to gather some galingale. He had seen some of the plants growing around the abbey pond and he wanted to use the roots in an infusion he was making to help a digestive disorder that was afflicting Brother Bernard. He'd described what the plant looked like and Nicholas had set off in search of it.

The abbey pond was situated behind the abbot's lodgings and was rarely visited. Its water was stagnant and weedy and had a rank odour – especially during the warm summer months. It had smelled bad today, Nicholas said, and having found and picked the reedy galingale, he had had no intention of loitering. But as he walked back round the pond, he had heard voices nearby in animated conversation.

'I am not interested in your petty silver and gold. It is power I seek – power and knowledge.'

It was Abbot Gregory who had spoken, and his words stopped Nicholas in his tracks.

('It was like when you overheard Brother Alban and Brother Symeon that night in the reredorter,' Nicholas told Thomas. 'I know I shouldn't have listened, but I couldn't help it.')

'With respect, Father Abbot, there is nothing petty about riches.' There was no mistaking the cool, measured tones of Brother Alban. 'Wealth *is* power.'

'Earthly power,' Father Gregory replied contemptuously. 'It is the realm of spirits I would control.'

For the next few minutes the two men discussed the merits of earthly and spiritual power. Brother Alban claimed that both could be achieved. He said that the abbey could become the most prosperous in the land, and Father Gregory the most influential abbot. When Father Gregory still seemed unconvinced, the prior reminded him that monasteries no longer received the respect and patronage they once had and their influence was dwindling. Even with the relics, Maundle's finances were in a less than healthy state. The increase in pilgrims, while bringing valuable income, also brought expenses. The abbey was in need of money – and Dr Langfell's experiments, if successful, offered rich rewards. The secrets of the philosopher's stone itself, the ability to turn base metals into gold, could be theirs, Brother Alban suggested with unusual excitement. It was too great an opportunity to be missed. Father Gregory expressed his concern that these 'financial' experiments would interfere with his quest for divine truths. Brother Alban assured him that this would not be so. The two elements of Dr Langfell's work were mutually beneficial.

Nicholas broke off his account and stared deep into Thomas's eyes. 'It was then that they spoke of your father,' he said solemnly.

'My father?' Thomas questioned. 'What of my father?'

'Brother Alban seeks to create gold from metal with the help of Doctor Langfell and his alchemy,' Nicholas explained. 'Your father needs gold to fashion his goods. It seems they have come to an arrangement.'

'An arrangement?' Thomas felt suddenly sick.

'Are you all right?' Nicholas asked.

Thomas nodded. 'Just tell me,' he murmured.

'Father Gregory didn't really want your father involved, but Brother Alban said his participation was vital. He will turn the gold into money.'

Thomas sat in silent thought for a moment before saying softly, 'Surely no man can turn ordinary metal into gold. It is just a myth.'

'Brother Alban certainly believes it,' Nicholas answered, 'and I suppose your father must too.'

Thomas shook his head. 'I find that incredible,' he said. 'He is not the sort of man to put his faith in myths.'

'Brother Alban must be very persuasive,' Nicholas countered, 'or perhaps it is Doctor Langfell.'

Thomas considered this. A picture formed in his head of Dr Langfell: dark, sinister, impressive – yes, he was sure he could be very persuasive.

'Father Gregory called him a necromancer,' Nicholas went on. 'He said Doctor Langfell was a master and a man of great learning in the ways of the spirit world.'

'What is a necromancer?' Thomas asked.

Nicholas shrugged. 'I don't know.'

Thomas sighed. Here was another mystery to unravel. 'Did Father Gregory say anything more?' he enquired.

Nicholas thought for a moment. 'He said something strange about Brother Alban. When Brother Alban was talking about his plans to make gold and money, Father Abbot warned him not to involve himself in any unlawful practices. "Do not forget why you are here, Brother," he said. "The king's gratitude is not boundless. Do not count on his agents protecting you a second time." Then he mentioned this name, Richard Lovell. He said that he might be Brother Alban's nemesis if he transgressed again – and that even his holiness's indulgences might not be enough to save him. What do you think he meant by that?'

Thomas shrugged. 'I don't know, but it does not surprise me that Brother Alban has a murky past.'

'No,' Nicholas agreed. 'I didn't hear much more. Brother Dominic called me. Brother Silvius had sent him to find me, worried that I would not be able to recognize the galingale.' Nicholas gave a rueful smile. 'He gave me a real fright. I thought I'd been discovered.'

'But you hadn't?'

'I don't think so. I moved away quickly as soon as I heard Brother Dominic's call.' Nicholas looked into Thomas's eyes again, but this time his gaze pulsed with excitement. 'But I did hear something else before I left,

Thomas.' In the brief pause his gaze grew more intense. 'There's going to be an important experiment tomorrow at midnight in Doctor Langfell's quarters.'

Thomas nodded. He stared into the empty fireplace. 'And I shall be there to witness it,' he said with quiet determination.

Uncle Jack bought the Racing Post *most days and he liked to have 'a flutter', as he called it. He even asked me to go down to the bookies for him once – only half in jest.*

'They'll never serve me,' I said. 'Besides, I don't approve of gambling.' I didn't either. I got that off Mum. I mean, Dad was no fan of gambling but Mum loathed it. She said it was a shameful waste of money. She didn't even like the lottery, though she conceded that at least the proceeds went to a good cause. Uncle Jack joked that one day they'd go to him and that would be a very good cause indeed. But he was serious about the lottery. He bought a lottery ticket every week. I'm not sure where he got the money from – Dad, I guess. 'If you don't buy a ticket, you can't win the lottery,' he said, as if that explained everything. Dad said he didn't want to win – having millions of pounds you hadn't earned would only bring unhappiness. Jack scoffed at that. Having millions would never bring him unhappiness

– it would transform his life for the better. Wealth brought influence and freedom – and power, he argued.

Mum sided with Dad. 'People waste their lives waiting to win the lottery instead of enjoying what they've got,' she said. 'We have to make the best of what we have. We only have one life and it's a short one.'

How right she was.

Chapter 22

Thomas found it hard to sleep that night. He lay awake for what seemed like hours listening to the sounds of the sleeping monks in the dormitory around him, and over it all the plaintive sighing of the wind in the eaves. He wondered if he'd ever sleep soundly again – he who used to be such a prodigious sleeper before he came to the abbey. He closed his eyes and tried to imagine himself back in his bedroom at home: the curved roof beams, the blue wall-hangings, the old oak chest, the animal skulls . . . But the skulls made him think about Dr Langfell and his experiments.

After chapter the next day, he asked Brother Martin what he knew of necromancers.

'Why do you ask?' the novice master quizzed him with uncharacteristic severity.

Thomas hesitated, considering his words carefully. 'I think my father may be involved with one.'

'Then you must pray that he will see the error of his ways. Necromancy is a black art and to be shunned by all Christian folk.' But what it was exactly, Brother Martin would not say.

Brother Luke, however, was more forthcoming. 'Brother Martin is right. Necromancy is a black art,' the librarian remarked when Thomas had told him of his brief conversation earlier. 'The word derives from the Greek words *nekros*, meaning dead, and *manteia*, meaning divination.' He explained that its practitioners believed that the disembodied spirits of the dead had superior knowledge about both past and future, and might communicate this to the living. The practice was generally condemned by the Church, though there were some within who felt it worthy at least of consideration. It *was* after all mentioned in the Holy Bible. 'I will show you the passage,' said the librarian. He limped across to his desk, where a beautifully illustrated Bible lay open. 'Now, let me see . . .' Next to the Bible was a pair of magnifying spectacles, which he put on as he bent over the desk searching for the right page, giving Thomas a full view of the back of his crown, around which his orange hair glowed in the lamplight like a halo. 'It's in Latin, of course. The Pope will not have us employ any other language, though I must confess in my humility that I do not entirely understand why a man should not be allowed to read Our Lord's words in his own tongue. But no doubt that day will soon come.' He peered at the page before him. 'Here we are. Samuel, Book One, Chapter Twenty-eight.'

Brother Luke proceeded to read the relevant passage, translating it into English so that Thomas would find it easier to understand. It was the story of King Saul, who, deserted by God and fearing the army of the Philistines, consulted a witch at Endor, commanding her to bring forth the spirit of King Samuel, which she did. Samuel was angry at being disturbed and he had a bleak message for his successor: on the following day the Philistines would defeat the Israelites in battle, and Saul and his sons would be killed.

'So much for necromancy,' Brother Luke concluded. He looked around at his beloved bookshelves. 'You will not find anything on the subject in this library,' he stated – almost regretfully, it seemed to Thomas. 'Though we have our share of books on esoteric matters – astrology, astronomy and the like.' The librarian reached up and pulled down a large tome. '*Ars Judiciaria Secundum Novem Judices*,' he read with relish. 'The Book of the Nine Judges. It contains the work of many esteemed writers, including Aristotle. It is a particular favourite of our Father Abbot.'

'Indeed?' Thomas said with interest.

Brother Luke gave Thomas a quizzical stare. 'Tell me, my son, what provokes this sudden fascination with necromancy?'

Just as he had earlier, Thomas hesitated, unsure how much to reveal. 'I believe – I believe Doctor Langfell may be a necromancer,' he said at last.

Brother Luke frowned. 'What cause have you to believe that?'

'I – I cannot say,' Thomas stuttered, feeling suddenly foolish. But to reveal how he knew what he knew would be to land Nicholas in trouble.

The librarian's eyes grew stern. 'Rumour is foolish and sinful, Thomas. Keep not its company.'

'I will not, Father,' Thomas muttered, feeling himself blush.

That day, it seemed to Thomas, lasted longer than any other he had known. He copied more of Father Eidric's wise words, practised psalm singing with Brother Bernard, ate a hearty dinner of charlet (the mixture of chopped meat, eggs and milk was one of his favourite dishes, but today he barely tasted it), dug in the kitchen garden, went into church for Vespers and then again for Compline. But at last the day was done. It was time for the monks to retire to bed – but not for Thomas, at least, to sleep. This is when his day was truly to begin.

Chapter 23

Nicholas insisted on joining Thomas, in spite of the latter's protestations. If they were caught, they could be in serious trouble, he said, and he didn't see why Nicholas should expose himself to that danger. It wasn't *his* father who was involved in the matter, after all. But now, walking through the dark and draughty cloisters, Thomas was pleased to have a companion. As day had turned to night, so his excitement had turned to apprehension at what he might discover.

It was a dark, windy, starless night. The clouds had been heavy all day, as if presaging a storm, but as yet it hadn't come. The two young monks made slow progress through the monastery, partly because of the blackness (they could not risk any form of light) but also because they were being careful not to make any undue noise, knowing that a simple stumble could undermine their whole enterprise.

They hardly dared breathe until, at last, they were out in the large courtyard in front of the abbey church, where they could rest a few moments before continuing. There were still lights showing in the guesthouse and the sound of voices. There was light too in the upper room of Dr Langfell's residence. The two novices made their way towards it.

The door to the gatehouse was locked, which was no surprise. Dr Langfell's activities had been conducted in secrecy since his arrival; he wasn't going to throw open his door now, when his experiments had reached such an apparently critical juncture. Thomas cast a glance at the thick mass of ivy that covered the walls.

'We'll have to climb up,' he whispered, reaching out his hand to grasp a doughty stem. He tugged at it gently and, satisfied that it was suitably stable, started to climb. Nicholas watched an instant or two, waiting until his friend was above the height of his head, and then he followed.

It was difficult going. There were few places for them to rest their feet, and their hands had to work hard to pull them upwards. Thomas's palms were chafed and sore by the time he'd reached halfway. His habit didn't help either. It was either caught up in the ivy leaves or tangled about his legs. But at last he reached the turret slot through which they'd seen the light shining. It was a ventilation hole rather than a window and had no glass in it. He peered in. At first he could see little but the back of Brother Alban. The prior's tall, broad-backed form obscured the rest of the room. But Thomas knew Father Gregory was in there, because he heard his voice.

'Is all ready?' he asked in his characteristically clipped tone.

'Almost,' said a deeper, more sonorous voice, which Thomas identified as Dr Langfell's. 'All we await is the storm.' As if on cue, the sky above Thomas started to rumble. An instant later, rain splattered the ivy leaves. Thomas pulled up his hood and Nicholas did the same. 'It is time for you to take your positions,' said Dr Langfell. 'And remember, you must not at any cost show yourselves or make a sound. The effects could be catastrophic.' He paused before adding theatrically, 'Not to say perilous.'

Thomas and Nicholas exchanged a quick, anxious glance, before returning their gaze to the slit once more. Brother Alban had moved now and was no longer in view – and nor was Father Gregory. But Dr Langfell was – and he cut an impressive figure. He wore a long black robe that reached to the floor, circled at the waist by a broad gold girdle bearing a list of strange words – *Ya, Aie* . . . There was more writing on his gold shoes, which were decorated with black crosses. On his head he wore a tall mitre-like hat of sand-coloured silk. In his hands he held a large book with a cross on the cover that might, Thomas thought, be a Bible. In front of the necromancer, on a round stone table, stood a copper tripod holding a glass dish smoking with incense; above him, hanging by a silver chain from the ceiling, a single lamp burned. A square had been carefully drawn in chalk on the floor around Dr Langfell and his table, and beyond the square were two circles. The space between the two circles was filled with chalked triangles and crosses.

If this scene had a striking effect on Thomas, what he saw next made such an impression that it was all he could do not to cry out. For at the commanding call of Dr Langfell, shambling out of the shadows, appeared Ambrose. He too was wearing a long black robe and his face bore the same odd smile as that evening when Thomas had seen him carving his unholy effigy in the cloisters. He was carrying a golden chalice in one hand and in the other, a golden plate like the paten used to hold the Host, though Thomas could not see what it actually contained for it was covered by a piece of embroidered linen edged with white lace.

Ambrose placed the chalice and the paten on the stone

table, on either side of the copper tripod. Then he stood inside the chalked square next to Dr Langfell. Lightning flashed. The rain fell harder now. Thomas could feel dampness against his skin as the water began to seep through his serge habit and the thin cotton tunic beneath. But he didn't allow his discomfort to distract him. His attention was totally drawn to what was happening inside the gatehouse.

The next time lightning flashed, Dr Langfell opened the book he was holding and began to read aloud in a deep chanting tone. The language in which he spoke was foreign to Thomas. It was neither English nor Latin – and neither did he think it was Greek (was it Arabic or Hebrew perhaps?). Ambrose meanwhile stepped up to the table and picked up the chalice once more. He advanced with it and sprinkled its contents (holy water? Thomas wondered) into the outer circle. Then he did the same in the inner circle, before returning to the square. It looked to Thomas like some kind of sanctifying ritual like the one performed by the brothers each Sunday in the cloisters.

The small room was now thick with the heady aroma of incense. Dr Langfell handed the heavy book to Ambrose. Then, closing his eyes, he lifted the covered paten into the air before him, chanting in the same strange language. Lightning flashed again and suddenly the necromancer opened his eyes wide and drew aside the linen cover from the paten. Thomas peered through the smoky gloom to try to see what was revealed there. He frowned and recoiled, exchanging a quick glance with Nicholas, whose perplexed expression he was sure mirrored his own: what lay on the paten was a severed tongue.

Dr Langfell's voice was louder now, commanding, as if he were summoning something forth. From the babble of his speech, intelligible words spouted: 'Vouchsafe to be present, o mighty spirit, conductor of the dead! Come forth, cry, speak, roar, bellow! Make your presence known unto me. May this tongue be your tongue and through this tongue your words be spoken. I call on you to appear before me!'

Suddenly the lamp above Dr Langfell flared, as if of its own accord. A terrible howl sounded in the tenebrous confusion. Then the howl became a wild and inhuman shrieking, as though some fierce beast were suffering dreadful torment. Thomas shivered and Nicholas shrank back. As he did so, his foot lost its resting place and he slipped down the wall through the ivy. At the same time he cried out involuntarily. His fall might have gone unremarked inside the gatehouse, but his cry did not. Dr Langfell's eyes were daggers of fury and they seemed to be aimed right at Thomas. 'Who dares to spy on the spirits? Reveal yourself!' he growled.

Thomas moved quickly, driven by terror. In an instant he was half sliding, half tumbling down the ivy, following Nicholas, who was now almost at the bottom. He could hear the sound of footsteps thudding down the stairwell inside the gatehouse and the agitated murmur of voices.

'Quick, Nicholas, we must move fast!' Thomas hissed. Hitching up their heavy, sodden habits, the two novices ran for their lives across the large outer courtyard. They didn't stop until they came to the west door of the abbey church. Lifting the latch, they pushed open the heavy oak door and slipped inside. As he closed the door, Thomas glanced back into the darkness and could just make out the shadowy figures of their pursuers barely fifty paces away.

'We must get to bed before they catch us,' he said urgently with an involuntary shudder. Nicholas nodded and led the way up the nave towards the north transept and the night stairs that would take them to the dormitory. There was something unfitting about running through this most sacred and solemn of places, Thomas felt, but they had no choice. As they reached the stairs and started to climb, they heard the clunk of the church door latch. In his haste, Nicholas tripped on one of the narrow stone steps, but luckily Thomas was on hand to steady him. Still, precious seconds were lost. Their pursuers would soon be upon them.

At the top of the stairs the novices went quickly to their respective beds. Thomas slipped off his shoes and fell onto his straw mattress. There was no time even to cast off his wet habit. He pulled the blanket up to his throat and closed his eyes as if in sleep. But there was no way that he *could* actually sleep. His heart was beating faster than a hunted stag's as he lay there, hearing the soft tread of footsteps ascending the night stairs, then moving slowly, quietly, through the dormitory. When they stopped by his bed, Thomas felt as if his breath had stopped too. He was terrified. There was a faint sound, as if someone were opening his lips, preparing to speak. *This is it*, thought Thomas with a surge of panic. *I have been discovered*. He shut his eyes tighter, and prayed.

He heard a foot slide across the floor. There was a brief, agonizing pause, then the footsteps went away.

When Thomas finally felt it safe to open his eyes, he saw that his shoes were no longer visible. Someone had hidden them from view beneath the edge of his blanket. But he was too exhausted now to consider who or why. He drew off his wet habit and lay down to sleep.

The first time, at the end of the service, I shook hands with Father Christopher at the church door. He asked me who I was and whether I was new to the area and if I'd enjoyed the service – and then he gave me a kind but penetrating gaze and said, 'You look sad, Liam.' I just shrugged, which was my usual response when anyone tried to get me to open up about my feelings. 'Would you like to talk about it?' he asked. But he didn't ask in that concerned but detached, phoney counsellor-type way that irritated me so much. No, he asked it like he was a friend, like he really meant it. So I nodded and, surprising myself rather, said 'Yes', and he invited me round to the vicarage the next day.

I'd expected him to be wearing robes and stuff like when he was in church, but he wasn't. He was wearing jeans and a black shirt and looked kind of normal – well, except for the dog collar. I guess he was about Dad's age, but he had a younger manner. He was tallish – around six foot – and big with a round cheruby face. He looked like someone who enjoyed laughing.

We sat in his study. It was full of books and papers – a bit like Dad's study really, except for the large wooden crucifix that hung on one wall. I gave him the background to what had happened with Mum and afterwards. I told him about the bereavement counsellors I'd seen and the therapist and how we just hadn't hit it off and what a waste of time it had been.

'Well, at least they pointed you in the direction of the

church,' Father Christopher commented wryly.

'Kind of,' I said. 'But I wouldn't have come if Dad hadn't been so against it.'

'So you came here to spite him?'

'Yeah, pretty much.' I explained my antagonism towards Dad, how I thought he'd just let Mum go like he didn't really care.

'I'm sure he does care,' Father Christopher said. 'Maybe he just doesn't know how to show it.'

'You can say that again,' I agreed.

'Maybe he just doesn't know how to show it,' he said again. He smiled. 'Poor joke. Sorry.'

I smiled anyway. It was good to talk to a professional person with a sense of humour.

I opened up more in that hour with Father Christopher than I had in all the various counselling and therapy sessions I'd had since Mum's death. In fact I revealed more to him than I had to anyone – even Uncle Jack. Uncle Jack was amusing and fun to be with, but somehow he wasn't the sort of person you confided your deepest emotions to. That just wasn't his thing. He didn't like to talk about anything too deep. Talking to Father Christopher was really like talking to a father – not my father, of course, I couldn't talk to him, but a normal father, one who could express his emotions and didn't turn his back on everything and bury his head in a lot of old bones. That sort of father.

We didn't talk about God at all until quite near the end of our conversation. He told me that his mother had died of cancer not long before, and although she had been a lot older than my mum, it had been a very difficult thing for him to cope with.

'It's odd,' he said. 'People expect you to be able to cope OK because you're a man of God, but it's just as painful as for anyone else. Losing someone you love is always intensely upsetting, even if you do believe in an afterlife.' He gave me one of those penetrating looks. 'Do you believe in an afterlife, Liam?'

I shrugged. 'To be honest,' I said, 'I don't even know if I believe in God.'

Father Christopher smiled. 'Mmm, well, I suppose that would be like putting the cart before the horse,' he said.

I asked him a question. 'How did you cope with your mum dying?' I wondered. It seemed a question worth asking, though I had no great expectations. No one else had been able to help me so far.

Father Christopher considered for a moment or two. 'I prayed a lot,' he said. 'I got lots of support and people were very kind to me, but I found prayer the greatest comfort. That's when I felt closest to my mother.'

'The power of prayer,' I remarked in a tone that made me

wince inside, because it sounded a bit too much like Dad.

'Yes, prayer can be powerful,' he agreed. 'But I'm not talking about lightning flashes or visions or sudden miracles; the power may simply lie in being quiet and still and voicing some of the concerns that we wouldn't otherwise find the time or opportunity to voice. That's how it was for me anyway.' He paused and looked at me thoughtfully. 'Would you like to try, Liam? We can pray now together if you'd like.'

'I wouldn't know how,' I said.

'I could say a prayer for you, if you like, to start things off,' Father Christopher offered. 'Then you can join in – or just stay silent. Whatever you like.'

'OK,' I said.

'I usually close my eyes when I pray,' he said, 'because I find it easier to focus my thoughts. But do as you please.'

I nodded.

Father Christopher closed his eyes and I closed mine, and after a few moments he said a simple, humble prayer, asking God to bring comfort in my time of grief. Then we sat in silence. I can't say I had any great revelation. I didn't suddenly see a light or anything, but I felt something – a sense of peace in my heart, of security, like there was someone who understood. It didn't last long but it was enough to make me go back to church the following

Sunday, and the one after that.

I wanted so much to believe in God because I wanted desperately for there to be an afterlife – a beautiful place where Mum could live on and be happy and where one day I could join her. How I prayed for that.

Chapter 24

The night took its toll on Nicholas. The next morning he woke up shivery and feverish and was unable to get out of bed. Brother Silvius examined him and gave him a warm infusion made from honey and spices. 'He needs warmth, peace and rest,' the infirmarian declared. 'As soon as he is a little stronger, we shall transfer him to the infirmary, where we can better care for him.' He turned his hale face towards Thomas and gave him an appraising stare. 'You look pale yourself, my son. Perhaps you too are in need of our ministrations.'

It was true, Thomas did not feel at his best: he was weary, his body ached and his palms were a mess of blisters and abrasions from his climb the night before. The prospect of spending some time in the infirmary was enticing, but there was far too much going on around him.

He did not want to miss out on any development. And developments there soon were.

Dr Langfell was present at chapter that morning. He sat beside Father Gregory, looking, Thomas thought, more sinister than ever as he glowered at the assembled monks. Thomas avoided his eyes, concentrating instead on the abbot. Not that there was any comfort to be found there, for Father Gregory was in the sternest of moods. He spoke once more of the important work that their visitor was undertaking and reiterated his former stipulation that on no account was he to be disturbed – or, he added with a steely glance at his fellow brethren, observed without his permission. Yet this instruction had been flouted the previous night. Some person or persons had climbed the wall of the inner gatehouse and interrupted the doctor at a vital point in his research. It was unforgivable – and he called upon the culprit to step forward now and receive his judgement.

An uncomfortable silence fell on the chapter house. It was a difficult moment for Thomas. The abbot was his spiritual father, his earthly master, and it was his duty to obey him. He should confess to what he had done. But he remembered Ambrose and how cruelly he had been punished. He did not believe either that Dr Langfell was a holy man. He was a necromancer who practised the black arts. The rituals Thomas had witnessed the previous night were surely dark, evil. He recalled the severed tongue, the terrible shrieking . . . Perhaps he was wrong. He was only a novice, after all. But he needed to talk to someone he could trust; someone whose opinion he respected entirely. He would confess, but not to the abbot and Brother Alban, here in the presence of Dr Langfell; he would do it in private to Brother Martin. If it was the novice master's judgement that he had sinned, then he would offer himself for chastisement – but he alone; he would not implicate Nicholas.

The abbot grew impatient at the monks' silence. He called once more for the culprit to confess. When there was still no response, he drew in a sharp breath and said gravely, 'Very well, if the culprit will not reveal himself by his own volition, we shall have to use other methods to uncover him.' He turned to his guest. 'Doctor Langfell, we would request your assistance.'

Dr Langfell assented with an almost imperceptible nod, then stood up and stepped forward. Whatever you felt about the man, Thomas thought, he had an astonishing presence. He towered over the abbot, but it wasn't just his height that gave him stature; there was an aura of power about him. He reached for a black velvet bag that hung from his doublet and, releasing the drawstring clasp, took out a phial which contained some kind of murky white oil. Then, raising one hand in a beckoning motion, he summoned Ambrose.

The gasps of surprise and confusion that met Ambrose's appearance were quelled by Father Gregory, who explained that the errant novice had been helping Dr Langfell in penance for his wrongdoing. For his part, Ambrose grinned his peculiar grin and said nothing. Dr Langfell commanded Ambrose to stretch out his hand in the direction of the chapter house's perpendicular window, so that it was touched by sunlight. Then he removed the stopper from the phial and poured the oil onto his assistant's fingernails, smearing it over them with his own finger. Now he began to chant in the same arcane language as the previous night, waving his hands over Ambrose's moistened nails as if performing some magical rite. It was a compelling, if chilling spectacle, which seemed to hold the whole company in thrall.

At last Dr Langfell ceased his chanting and dropped his hands.

'Now,' the necromancer intoned, 'let the guilty one be discovered. Look closely at your nails. Whose face do you see reflected there?' Ambrose stared open-mouthed, trance-like, at his oil-smeared nails. Then, finally, he looked up, the weird grin returning. He lifted his hand with one finger outstretched as if to point out the 'guilty' party. Thomas held his breath as the finger slowly, inexorably moved in his direction. But it was brought to a sudden halt by Brother Bernard.

'Stop!' he cried, getting to his feet. 'My Lord Abbot, I must protest. Onychomancy is an abominable necromantic practice and should have no place in a house of God.'

His outburst received supportive murmurs from some of the monks around him – including, Thomas noted, Brother Martin and Brother Luke.

Father Gregory met the precentor's complaint with cold disdain. 'Disobedience, defiance, dishonesty – these should have no place in a house of God, Brother, I am sure you would agree. But they are among us. What harm does Doctor Langfell in helping to unmask the perpetrator of these sins?'

'With respect, Lord Abbot, two wrongs do not make a right,' Brother Bernard insisted. 'And using a holy psalm in the ungodly rite of nail divination is sin indeed.'

Dr Langfell's lips formed themselves into a thin smile. 'Bravo, Brother, I see you know your Hebrew,' he said with forced mirth. 'But it seems you know little of my art or you would not call it abominable or ungodly. I believe in God as ardently as you. Might I draw your attention to the writings of Ivo of Chartres – you know of him, I trust?'

Brother Bernard nodded. 'Of course. Brother Luke has some of his writings in the library.'

'Then you may well be familiar with his great work *De Divinitionibus et Incantationibus*, in which he claims the authority of Augustine of Hippo himself in proclaiming that divination is not anything to do with evil, but a human concern with the doubtful, and a means of indicating the divine will.'

Now Brother Silvius joined the argument. 'You know full well, Doctor Langfell,' he said, 'that the Holy Church decries necromancy and all such practices on pain of excommunication. Brother Bernard is right: onychomancy is indeed a sin and—'

'Enough!' Father Gregory interjected, ending the debate with a peremptory wave. 'There are tasks to be done. This meeting is ended.' His eyes were cool and hard as stone. 'But be assured, Brothers, this matter is not concluded.'

CHAPTER 25

After chapter, Thomas revealed all to Brother Martin. He told him everything that had happened the night before (although omitting Nicholas's role in the proceedings), as well as the conversation that Nicholas had overheard between Father Gregory and Brother Alban. The novice master was deeply concerned. 'You should have spoken to me before this, Thomas,' he said sombrely. 'This Doctor Langfell is a dangerous man and you might have put yourself in great peril last night. Who knows what evil he might have conjured had he not been disturbed? This is a very serious matter – a very serious matter indeed.'

Brother Martin told Thomas that he had been right not to 'confess' in chapter, though his scruples about not doing so also did him credit. 'It is our duty under the rule of Benedict to obey our abbot, but it is also the duty of our abbot to lead with wisdom and compassion – as Father Eidric was ever wont to do. Father Gregory, to the chagrin of all of us who should serve him, has lost his way.' A deep frown scored his pockmarked forehead. 'We must pray for guidance.' He sighed and looked down at his sandaled feet for a moment or two. Then, looking up with an air of sadness, he said, 'It must pain you, Thomas, that your father is involved in this affair.'

Thomas nodded. 'Yes, Father,' he murmured. Saying the word, it struck him that he had numerous fathers now – yet only one whom he could truly trust. His own father had lied to him, his spiritual father had betrayed his order; only Brother Martin was steadfast – but not without cost. It seemed to Thomas that the novice master had greyed considerably over the past months since Abbot Eidric's death – not just his hair but his whole complexion. He had the air of a man carrying an intolerable burden. If only *he* had been elected abbot, Thomas thought. How much more suited to the post he was than Father Gregory – and he wondered momentarily whether it might not have been the novice master who had hidden his shoes the night before. Might he have been roused by the activity in the dormitory and, seeing the incriminating evidence against his novice, acted to conceal it? It seemed unlikely, but who else would do such a kind deed? None of his pursuers, certainly. It was yet another mystery . . .

After High Mass, Thomas returned to the dormitory to see how Nicholas was faring, but his friend was no longer in his bed. Thomas found him in the infirmary. He was very pale and his deep-set eyes were listless and watery. He managed a smile when Thomas called his name, but it was a weak smile that quickly faded. Thomas was very worried, but Brother Silvius did not seem unduly concerned.

'It's just a common ague,' he reassured Thomas; 'not the sweating sickness or anything like that. Nicholas has caught a chill but he is young and strong; with rest and care, he will be fine.'

Thomas was comforted by these words, but still he felt a sense of guilt that it was his venture the night before that had caused Nicholas's sickness. He wasn't allowed to dwell on this for long, however, for the infirmarian sent him off to the herb garden to collect herbs for various remedies and infusions he was concocting.

Later, after dinner, Thomas spent time in the library with Brother Luke, as had become his routine. The librarian studied the homily by Abbot Eidric that Thomas was copying and gave a heavy sigh. 'What would our late abbot make of all that is happening here? He must be turning in his grave at Father Gregory's shenanigans.' He shook his large head despairingly. 'You were right about Doctor

Langfell being a necromancer – though I do not know why you should have suspected this.'

Thomas told the librarian about the conversation Nicholas had overheard by the abbot's lodgings. With all that had happened since, he was confident his friend's eavesdropping would not bring him any great censure. Thomas also repeated to Brother Luke his account of the previous night's events.

Brother Luke was appalled. 'The Lord knows, I am not one for upholding foolish prejudices and I have always advocated the pursuit of learning, but Father Gregory goes too far. Brother Alban also.'

'It would seem so from what Nicholas heard the abbot say about him,' Thomas proposed. 'Do you know of Richard Lovell, Father, and why he should be Brother Alban's nemesis?'

'I know the name Lovell,' the librarian stated. 'The Lovells are an old and noble Yorkist family. But I do not know this Richard Lovell. As to why he should be our brother prior's nemesis, I have no idea, my son.' Brother Luke smiled wanly. 'It is one of the blessings of this place that we are ill-informed of the intrigues of the courtly world.'

They fell silent for a moment or two, then, 'What will happen now?' Thomas asked.

'Brother Bernard wishes to write a complaint to the bishop. It is a drastic measure but I think it may be the only one left to us.' Brother Luke sighed again. 'It is a terrible thing for a house to be at strife with itself.'

Brother Luke was able to clarify some of the things that Thomas had seen and heard. Dr Langfell's use of Hebrew, for instance. 'Many of these occultists believe Hebrew to have a magical power because it was the language in which the Bible was first written,' he explained. 'The psalm that Doctor Langfell recited today in his divination was psalm one hundred and nineteen. It is a favourite among necromancers because each verse begins with a different letter of the Hebrew alphabet.' He also informed Thomas about the various shapes and figures he had seen chalked on the gatehouse floor – the circle was held to have magical qualities, while triangles and crosses were holy symbols. Together they acted like a shield, protecting the necromancer from the spirit he summoned.

'Do you think that Doctor Langfell really did summon forth a spirit?' Thomas asked.

'I suspect that Doctor Langfell is a charlatan. There are many such, who would exploit men's greed for riches and power.'

'But the shrieking?'

'Ambrose probably. He has a voice of great virtuosity.'

Thomas recalled that that was true. Certainly he was a very talented singer.

'But what about the severed tongue?' Thomas pondered aloud.

'Body parts are not difficult to come by these days.'

'Yes, but . . .' Thomas hesitated, wondering whether he should voice a suspicion that had been nagging at him all day. 'It's just that . . . Matthew Cundulus had his tongue cut out and his heart. And . . .'

'Yes?'

'What if Doctor Langfell was responsible for his death?'

Brother Luke puffed out his cheeks and raised his fiery eyebrows. 'Necromancy is one thing, Thomas, but murder? That would be a damnable crime indeed.'

Thomas pictured the hateful stare the necromancer had aimed his way the night before. Yes, he could believe Dr Langfell capable of murder.

'There is so much that confuses me still,' he uttered sorrowfully.

'No doubt you are worried about your father's part in all this,' Brother Luke suggested. Thomas nodded. 'Then perhaps you need to speak to him.'

Thomas considered this as he sat in the cloister later. He was afraid of Dr Langfell, he was intimidated by Father Gregory and he didn't trust Brother Alban; that only left his father. Right now he didn't trust him either, but he was the most approachable of the four. Perhaps Brother Luke was right. Perhaps he should go home and speak to his father. He'd ask Brother Martin about it. If he had no objections, then hopefully he would intercede on Thomas's behalf with the abbot, who alone had the power to permit such absences.

But it was not to be, for that evening, at supper, the abbot issued an edict that no brother was to leave the monastery until further notice.

CHAPTER 26

Nicholas was still feverish the next day but there were periods when he felt well enough to talk – or to listen at any rate. Thomas brought him up to date with events in the chapter house and his discussions with Brother Martin and Brother Luke.

'Do you really think Doctor Langfell might have had something to do with Matthew Cundulus's murder?' Nicholas asked.

Thomas shrugged. 'Perhaps,' he said.

'But why?'

'I don't know,' Thomas admitted. He sighed. 'There's so much I don't know. But I do know one thing: Doctor Langfell gives me the shivers.'

'This chill gives me the shivers,' Nicholas remarked wryly. 'But that doesn't make it a murderer.'

'No,' Thomas agreed. 'But that tongue . . .'

'Matthew Cundulus was murdered months ago,' Nicholas countered.

'I know. But it was after he came here. What if he were murdered *because* he came here, because of what he found?'

'The mushrooms?'

'Yes. Or—?' Thomas stopped as a new thought came to him, a memory. 'What if it wasn't what he found, but who he saw?' Nicholas looked at his friend blankly. 'Matthew Cundulus saw someone in the courtyard that day,' Thomas continued, 'someone he was very surprised to see there. "What in Jehovah's name is he doing here?" he said. Well, what if that person was Doctor Langfell? He must have had meetings with Father Gregory before he moved in.'

'It could have been anyone, Thomas – an old friend, perhaps, or a former patient. So many different people seek hospitality here.'

'I know,' Thomas sighed. 'I am clutching at straws.'

Nicholas looked at his friend pityingly, as if it were *he* who was the sick one. 'There is one way of finding out who stayed here when,' he said. 'The hospitality book. All pilgrims sign the hospitality book when they lodge in the guesthouse. Brother Ignatius keeps it. You should ask him to show it to you.'

Thomas's spirits lifted at once. 'Of course!' he cried. 'Thanks, Nicholas!' Nicholas smiled and shivered. Thomas pulled the blanket around him. 'I'd better leave you to rest,' he said.

Later that morning Thomas visited the guesthouse and asked Brother Ignatius if he might look at the hospitality book. Brother Ignatius was a very large man, with a red face and an often surly manner, arising in no small measure from the acute gout that afflicted him. It was an irony that few failed to perceive that he should be responsible for hospitality. Thomas's request did little to improve his temper. He was busy, he snapped, and had no time for such trifling concerns. He softened a little, however, when Thomas offered to help him with his chores. And when the young novice had made a trip to the abbey well and returned with a brimming pail of water, Brother Ignatius became altogether more amenable, though before showing Thomas the hospitality book he still demanded to know why he wished to see it. Thomas made up some excuse about trying to trace the owner of a lost item, and as he leafed through the pages of the book, he was struck by how easy he found it to lie these days – or if not to lie, then at any rate not to reveal the truth.

He could not remember the exact date on which Matthew Cundulus had visited, but he knew the month in which it had taken place and leafed through the appropriate pages. He was lucky the visit had been before the summer influx of pilgrims, so the number of entries per day was relatively few. The search didn't take him long. He found what he was seeking under the heading 'Nineteenth of May'. His finger trembled as it lighted on the name he'd been looking for: Dr Stefan Langfell. So, he had been here! And he and Matthew Cundulus had known one another, Thomas was sure of it. As he walked back to the church for Nones, however, his sense of satisfaction dissipated in sudden apprehension at what his discovery might signify. He felt overwhelmed by a knowledge of things that were too immense for his age and position.

Not for the first time, the service restored his spirits. As he sat in his seat, and heard the huge church resonate around him with the transcendent singing of the monks, a community in melodious unison, it seemed to Thomas that all that had happened and was still happening – the plots, the clandestine conversations, the deaths and black arts – was inconsequential, dreamlike. Everything was, in comparison to the grandeur and majesty of God. Nothing could sully or destroy this wondrous vision of stone and wood and glass, not even with the dust and grime of the building works.

* * *

In the time between Nones and Vespers, Thomas helped Brother Martin (who had taken over the sacristan's duties since the death of Brother Symeon), clearing, cleaning and storing the vessels and vestments. Then he went to the library to continue his illustration of Father Eidric's homilies. But before he could make a start, Brother Luke sent him to the warming room to fetch a new supply of ink. It was stored there, above the fireplace, to keep it from freezing in the winter. Not that there was a fire today, despite the inclement weather. It was still too early in the season.

Thomas was in the process of inspecting the shelf in search of the various inks the librarian had requested when he heard the door latch rattle behind him. He started slightly and turned to see Brother Alban.

'You start like a guilty man, Thomas,' said the prior coolly. 'Not with cause, I hope.'

'No, Father,' Thomas muttered. He explained his purpose.

'No guilt then,' Brother Alban concluded. His face was so inexpressive that Thomas found it impossible to read. 'And yet . . .' The words hung accusingly in the air.

'Father?' Thomas queried.

'Are you in the habit of taking strolls by night in the rain?'

Thomas shook his head.

'Yet last night your shoes were soaked through. The floor was wet with them.'

Thomas felt his face flush. So it had been the prior who had kicked his shoes beneath his bed!

'I have no need of nail divination to know you were outside Doctor Langfell's residence last night, Thomas,' the prior continued coolly. He considered the novice with his shrewd, dark eyes, as if he were appraising an uncertain transaction. 'You do not deny it then?'

'No,' said Thomas. 'I have already confessed to Brother Martin.'

'But not to our Father Abbot; yet it is surely your duty to do so.'

'I was . . . confused,' Thomas admitted – and he still was. Why had Brother Alban chosen to hide the evidence of his 'crime' the night before – and why had he not exposed him?

'Confusion is no excuse, Thomas. The rule of Benedict is absolute in its demand of obedience to the abbot – and equally absolute about the penalties for disobedience. As you know, Father Gregory is not a man to take such a transgression lightly.'

Thomas shivered anew at the memory of what had happened to Ambrose.

'You disturbed an important experiment,' Brother Alban continued. 'Doctor Langfell was on the brink of an immense discovery.'

'Doctor Langfell is a necromancer.'

'And?'

'Necromancy is a black art, a sin.'

Brother Alban smiled faintly. Everything about him was so economical, Thomas thought. It struck him too how similar he was in height and physique to Dr Langfell. Each had dark eyes, yet while the prior's were unremittingly icy, the necromancer's were smouldering fires. 'Tell me, Thomas,' Brother Alban enquired, 'do you believe killing is a sin?'

'Of course!' Thomas responded vehemently. ' "Thou shalt not kill" is one of Our Lord's sacred commandments.'

'Yet the Crusaders did just that and we call them holy.'

'They killed the heathen in faith and righteousness, with the Holy Church's blessing,' Thomas countered.

'They killed nonetheless.' The prior made an inexpansive gesture with his right hand. 'And rightly so. The ends justify the means. They say necromancy is a sin, yet Doctor Langfell's experiments promise us wealth without which we may soon be unable to carry out our good works. Then who will feed the poor and the needy?'

'But . . .' Thomas struggled for words.

Brother Alban wasn't interested in his reply. 'I did not come here to discuss matters of theological nicety with you, Thomas,' he said. 'I need your assistance.'

'My assistance?'

'Yes. In a matter concerning your father. The abbot and I have been in consultation with him about certain mutually beneficial concerns. Of late, however, he has been – how can I express it? – unsupportive.'

'And what can I do to help?'

'You can write a letter to him, stressing the significance to the monastery of Doctor Langfell's work and the necessity of his support for it.'

Thomas returned the prior's cool stare in kind. 'And what if I don't wish to help?'

'And not do what is best for this house?' Brother Alban expressed his incredulity with the merest twitch of one eyebrow. 'I cannot believe you would be so mean spirited. But of course, should that be your position, I would feel obliged to inform the abbot of your exploits last night.' Though it was spoken with no force, there was no mistaking the threat.

It was clear now to Thomas why Brother Alban had not exposed him: it had been to further his own ends. But perhaps there was a way Thomas's own purposes could be served. 'I won't write a letter to my father,' he said decisively. 'I will only speak to him in person.'

'But, as you well know, the abbot's edict makes that impossible.'

Thomas shrugged. 'Then so be it. You must do what you will.'

Brother Alban's cool eyes revealed a hint of admiration. 'It might be possible to arrange,' he conceded. He considered a moment. 'Be at the gate ten minutes after Compline. You will find it unlocked. But you must be back inside the monastery by Matins.' He turned to leave, then turned back again. 'And, Thomas, this mission must be successful. The abbot is in no mood to brook further hindrance to our enterprise, and nor am I. As for Doctor Langfell, well, let us just say that he is not a man to be vexed by anyone – living or' – he paused momentarily for emphasis – 'dead.'

Dad and I constantly goaded each other. Every meal time was a skirmish between the two of us, with Uncle Jack trying to act as peacemaker.

Dad hated my new links with the church. He said Father Christopher was a dangerous man – all religious people were – peddling their unfounded and bigoted beliefs that were no more than superstition. 'It's just a crutch,' he said dismissively.

'Well, maybe that's what I need right now,' I said.

'Crutches are for moral weaklings,' Dad countered. 'Life's difficult and tough and brutish and you have to face the fact. No amount of happy clapping and hallelujahing can change that.'

'Thanks for those reassuring words,' I sneered.

'I'm just telling you the truth, Liam – not some ludicrous fantasy like they'll spin you down at that church.'

'You call it ludicrous fantasy. To them it's real.'

'Perhaps you should agree to disagree,' Uncle Jack interjected. 'Why not let Liam go to church if that's what he wants, Will? What harm can it do?'

'All the harm in the world,' Dad muttered darkly. 'All the harm in the world.'

The truth was I liked and respected Father Christopher more than Dad. He was easy to talk to and very pleasant and he seemed to genuinely care about me and how I was feeling in a way that Dad never seemed to have done since Mum had died. There were many times when I'd longed for him to put his arm around me and hug me and say something loving like he had when I was younger. But he never had done – and it had got to the stage now where I would have rejected any such show of affection. We lived like enemies in the same house. That was another of the attractions of the church – it got me away from the house where I'd started to feel like a prisoner.

When I was in church I felt like I was part of a family. I liked having all those people around me – and they were all so nice. They'd ask me how I was, make conversation, smile. I liked the singing too. Sometimes, when the choir was singing a response or an anthem, it was like the sound was tangible, like arms lifting me up, and I'd feel suddenly, fleetingly, very happy. At other times, though, the robes and rituals and strange phrases – 'begotten not made', 'incarnate by the Holy Ghost' – made me shiver. In those moments I'd see it all with Dad's eyes and be kind of horrified. It would all seem so alien and, well, kind of scary. But then I'd look up at that beautiful stained-glass window above the altar, stare right into it until I felt calm again. The window pictured the Virgin Mary, but what I saw was Mum.

Chapter 27

It was an odd feeling to be walking through this town that for so long had been his home, no longer as an inhabitant but as a visitor, an outsider. It surprised him how quickly he had become estranged from the world beyond the abbey walls. Everything seemed to be very much the same, and yet he no longer felt the same way about it. For a start, he found the smell of the place repugnant. The rank odour of human and animal ordure was so strong that even the pungent smell that still lingered in the air from the carcasses that hung by day outside the butchers' shops in The Shambles was a welcome relief. As he passed along that street, he was struck by how cramped the buildings were, something he'd never really remarked when he'd lived here; the monastery seemed roomy by comparison. The thin wooden houses leaned across the narrow cobbled street almost as if they were reaching out to touch one another. And over them all, grand, enormous, magnificent, like some omnipotent lord, loomed the town's great cathedral, the Minster.

Thomas walked on past the heaving taverns, full of row and clamour, and the sound that had become foreign to him now – raucous laughter. Laughter of any kind was rarely to be heard within the confines of the monastery (except among the late-night revellers in the guesthouse), but it was a long while since Thomas had heard such loud, uninhibited expressions of amusement. It reminded him of his father's hall, on the frequent occasions when he entertained wealthy clients and those he hoped would soon become his clients. This in turn made Thomas think about Dr Langfell. His room had been lit up again tonight when Thomas crossed the courtyard and slipped out through the unlocked gate at the side of the abbey gatehouse. At this very moment, no doubt, he was engaged in some nefarious experiment, assisted by the hapless Ambrose. Poor, dim-witted, ill-used Ambrose, who'd been saved by Father Eidric only to be pushed down into the pit again by his successor. Thomas was determined that *he* would not have the same fate. He would do all he could – with God's help – to come through these dark days with his soul unsullied, though he well knew it would not be easy.

At last he reached the passageway that led through to the courtyard at the back of his father's house. He hesitated for a moment. Behind him, a horse and cart clattered by down the otherwise silent, empty street. His father would be in bed by now and would not appreciate being woken. He would be in a foul mood. He might easily refuse to answer any of Thomas's questions. He might . . . But it was too late for all that now. Thomas straightened his habit and walked on.

It was Robin who answered his knocking. The servant's initial truculence soon turned to astonished delight on registering the visitor's identity.

'Master Thomas!' he exclaimed. 'What brings you here – and so late at night?'

Thomas explained that he had an urgent need to speak with his father.

'But the master is abed,' Robin blurted. 'He'll not take kindly to being woken. Can it not wait until the morning? I can prepare your old bed—'

'I can't stay, Robin. I must be back at the abbey tonight. But I must see my father.'

'I shall go and call him presently,' said the servant. 'But let me get you something to eat and drink while you wait.'

Thomas shook his head. 'Just fetch my father, please,' he beseeched. 'I shall wait for him in the parlour.'

He followed the flustered servant up the stairs and let himself into the parlour. This was the room where his father conducted most of his business when he wasn't in his shop. This was the room where he had entertained Dr Langfell. Thomas was weary from his long walk but he felt too agitated to sit down. The window shutters were closed and the room was gloomy in the flickering light from the candlestick that Robin had given him. But as he looked around, he pictured everything as clearly as if it were illuminated by bright sunlight: the wooden writing slope, with inkwells hollowed from the tips of cow horns; the red oak chest that contained the family's finest linen; the inviting settle and high-backed chair; the small polygonal table and the majolica jug with an image of a bird in black and blue that stood on it; the dyed red and green striped woven hangings suspended from the ceiling by big brass tenterhooks . . . Thomas took in all these familiar things but found no comfort in them. Indeed, their familiarity made him feel even more estranged, apart, alien.

He succumbed at last to the lure of the settle, sitting down to rest his tired legs. But no sooner had he done so than there was a commotion outside and the parlour door flew open. His mother appeared.

'Thomas!' she cried happily. 'Thomas, my darling!' She ran across the room and embraced him.

The reunion was quickly interrupted by a peremptory cough, and Thomas looked up to see his father standing in the doorway in his nightcap and gown, with the sourest of expressions on his face. 'And what, in the Devil's name, do you mean by this?' he growled.

One night I woke up to the sound of sobbing. I thought at first that I was dreaming. Then I thought about Mum. She used to cry. Sometimes I'd come in from school and find her sitting at the kitchen table, tears slipping down her face, dripping onto the table.

'What's wrong, Mum?' I'd say. I'd sling my bag down and put my arms around her. 'What's wrong?' But she'd never say. I'd hear her sobbing in her room too, and that really broke my heart. I couldn't bear it. I'd open her door and hurry in to try to comfort her. 'It's all right, Mum,' I'd say, but how could I know if it was or not when I didn't know what 'it' was?

But it wasn't Mum sobbing tonight, because she was dead – and I didn't believe in ghosts. I got up and walked to the door. The sobbing stopped, then started again. It was coming from my parents' room. I shivered because, well, irrational as it was, I suddenly thought, What if it *is* a ghost? *I wanted to see Mum again, but – a ghost? I didn't think I could cope with that. The sobbing stopped and started, quiet and desolate. I couldn't ignore it.*

I walked along the landing and opened my parents' bedroom door. I went in and stood motionless for a moment, frowning, as I tried to take in what I saw. Dad was huddled on the floor at the foot of the bed, clutching something to his chest. It was he who was sobbing.

'Dad?' I enquired softly.

He lifted his head slightly and I saw it was Mum's nightgown he was clutching. His eyes were raw with misery.

'I couldn't save her,' he said. 'She wouldn't let me. No one could save her.' He sobbed again but without a sound, as though the pain had taken his voice away.

It was the only time I'd ever seen Dad cry and he never has since.

CHAPTER 28

Thomas faced his father, who sat stiff-backed in his chair, his pink face querulous and hostile. He made Thomas sit a little away from him, complaining that he reeked ('Do you monks never wash?' he grumbled). It was just the two of them now – his mother having been dismissed after the initial greetings.

'Well, now,' said his father bitterly, 'perhaps you would be kind enough to explain what brings you knocking at my door at this unearthly hour?' He scowled. 'Indeed, what brings you here at all. I was not aware that young novices had dispensation to wander the world by night.'

'I come on abbey business,' said Thomas, not allowing himself to be intimidated by his father's overbearing manner. 'Prior Alban sent me.'

His father snorted. 'That gullible, grasping fool. What does he want of me now?'

Instead of answering the question, Thomas posed one of his own: 'What business do you have with Doctor Stefan Langfell?' he demanded.

For a moment Thomas's father gaped at him and appeared quite unable to speak, as astonished evidently as Thomas was himself by the brusque tone of the question. Certainly Thomas had never once dared speak to his father in such a way before. Then the goldsmith threw up his hands in irritation. 'What a preposterous and insolent question,' he blustered.

'Yet you cannot deny that he was here once and you visited him at the abbey,' Thomas persisted.

His father leaned back in his chair. His face relaxed a little. 'It's true the man was here once,' he admitted. 'But he's no more a doctor than you or I – unless they grant doctorates for quackery these days. He may call himself Doctor Stefan Langfell now, but his name is Wat Snyder. Well, that is the name he went by when he came here uninvited a couple of years back, calling himself an alchemist and trying to persuade me to take him into my business.'

'But you did not.'

'Of course not. The man was a mountebank, a knave, and I sent him packing. He tried the same ruse on other goldsmiths. Then he took to claiming he had divine healing powers and fell foul of the authorities. He was arrested for necromancy, tried and found guilty. Somehow he managed to escape from prison and cheat the hangman.'

Thomas was still not satisfied. 'But you did visit him at the abbey. I saw you.'

'You may well have seen me at the abbey, but I never went to visit that impostor. I was summoned by the abbot – or rather that rogue of a prior – to evaluate some precious ornaments. When I arrived, I was told of some brilliant stratagem they had for creating gold. They wanted me to meet the man responsible – a man of great art and learning, they assured me. Well, I recognized Snyder the moment I saw him and that was it. I would have nothing to do with the business.'

'Prior Alban believes you can be persuaded otherwise.'

'Prior Alban is a fool – and quite possibly a heretic also. I am no theologian but I cannot believe it to be right for a man of the Church to be meddling in necromancy.'

'But you have not reported Langfell.'

Thomas's father sighed. 'No. But only for your mother's sake. It would break her heart to see any scandal brought on the abbey. She still believes it to be a place of virtue and sanctity.'

'And so it is,' Thomas assured him, although not with

great conviction. He quickly changed the subject. 'Did you know Matthew Cundulus, Father?' he asked in a softer tone.

Thomas's father snorted once more. 'That popinjay!' he exclaimed. 'I never met the man but I knew of him. He was a man with lofty friends but dangerous enemies. I cannot say his end surprised me.'

'Do you know if Stefan Langfell – I mean, Wat Snyder – was acquainted with him?'

'Well, I should certainly think so,' his father declared. 'Doctor Cundulus was one of the main witnesses for the prosecution at Snyder's trial. He denounced Snyder as a false physician, a quack – as if he would know.'

Thomas immediately came to the defence of the dead physician. 'Matthew Cundulus was no quack, Father,' he proclaimed. 'I saw him practise. He was a man of great knowledge and wisdom, I am sure of it.'

'Hmm, well,' huffed his father, 'all I am sure of is that I am missing my sleep. You monks may not have to worry about earning a living but we guildsmen do – and that is no easy matter in these uncertain times. I hear that the king gave that explorer fellow John Cabot ten guineas for discovering some godforsaken country on the other side of the world; he would better have spent the money on sorting out the godforsaken country on his own doorstep, namely

Scotland. They say the Scots are getting ready to march south again and wreak havoc – and, as usual, we law-abiding citizens will be the ones to foot the bill.'

Thomas said nothing, reminded once more of how detached he had become from this outside world of exploration and war. Yet, he reflected, was there not strife enough within the abbey walls?

His father poured a cup of wine for himself and one for Thomas.

'These are difficult and dangerous times, Thomas,' he said, echoing Matthew Cundulus's warning, adding, with unusual solicitude, 'You are better off within the cloister.'

Thomas thought about this as he walked through the dank darkness on his way back to the monastery. Was he better off? Spiritually perhaps; but he was hardly safer. There had been two violent deaths in the short time he had been at the abbey – three if you counted Matthew Cundulus. But was Dr Langfell or Wat Snyder his murderer? He certainly had strong motives for committing the crime: revenge for denouncing him at his trial; anxiety that the physician had recognized him at the abbey and would alert the authorities. Yes, Langfell was still very much the chief suspect in Thomas's eyes. And yet something his father had said just before, as Thomas stood on the threshold, still warm from his mother's parting embrace, had muddied the waters. As he prepared to depart, Thomas had suddenly recalled a question that he had forgotten to ask.

'Do you know the name Richard Lovell?' he had enquired now.

'Of course,' his mother had replied at once. The Lovells were an old York family, she explained, confirming what Brother Luke had said. They had been valued customers of Thomas's father for many years. Richard Lovell was their son – or had been. He had died in suspicious circumstances soon after Henry had come to the throne. Here his father had taken up the story. Richard Lovell, it was said, had been poisoned and the deed had been done at the king's behest, for Lovell was a Yorkist sympathizer and no friend of the Tudors. His death was never investigated and the man believed to have been responsible for the poisoning disappeared. Some said he went abroad; others that he had entered a monastery. There was an ironic smile on the face of Thomas's father as he continued, 'This may interest you, Thomas. The physician who tended Lovell and diagnosed the poisoning was your friend – that gadfly Matthew Cundulus.'

Dad had little time for doctors – well, GPs anyway. I heard him remark once that they were jacks of all trades and masters of none. I don't know if he'd always felt that way or if it was because he thought they'd failed him and Mum when she'd got ill after having me. She had very bad post-natal depression and Dad felt that the medical profession (his phrase, as if somehow they had all been involved in Mum's treatment) had been unsympathetic and inadequate. She'd had to go into hospital with me for a few weeks. They put her on anti-depressants, which she took, on and off, for the rest of her life. I hadn't known about that as a child, and she was very good at hiding her depression, but as I got older I became more aware of her mood swings. I started to recognize it in her face – an anxious look in her eyes, a heavy quietness about her that wasn't at all peaceful; quite the opposite. When it was really bad, she'd hide away in her room as much as possible.

It was only about a year ago that Dad had actually talked to me about Mum's condition – that she suffered from depression. I guess I knew there was something wrong but I just thought Mum was a very anxious person. There were whole periods – months and months sometimes – when she was fine. I suppose that's when the drugs were working. I don't know if Dad ever would have talked to me about it if it hadn't been for that night I'd had to call the ambulance.

Dad was away at a dig, so it was just Mum and me at home. When I got back from school, I called out to Mum as I usually did. But there was no reply. I went upstairs to see if she was in her room and found her there, slumped on the bed. I thought at first that she was just asleep, but then I saw the empty pill bottle on the cabinet by her bed – and an empty bottle of vodka next to it. I got really scared.

I rushed over to Mum and shook her and tried to rouse her. She was conscious but not coherent. She just sort of whimpered. She kept muttering 'Sorry' over and over like a mantra in one of those cults we learned about in RS. By now I was seriously scared and panicky. But I had enough presence of mind to phone the emergency services and get them to send an ambulance – though I don't really recall doing it.

They took Mum to hospital and pumped her stomach and she was OK. Dad was home by then. He was furious with Mum. I couldn't believe that. I was just so relieved that she was OK and wasn't going to die, but not Dad. He was really angry that she'd done what she'd done: 'What about Liam?' he said. 'Didn't you think about him?'

'She couldn't help it,' I defended Mum. 'It doesn't matter about me.' But Dad wouldn't have it.

Later, when he talked to me about what had happened, he said that what Mum had done had been a cry for attention. She hadn't meant to kill herself. He understood that she was feeling bad, that the depression had really taken hold, but she shouldn't have got me involved. It was inexcusable, he said.

But I didn't agree. I'd have excused Mum anything. Anything at all. And I still do. Not that there's anything to excuse, is there?

CHAPTER 29

Thomas was exhausted. He'd had barely an hour's sleep, snatched between Matins and Lauds, and he was aching from his long walk to and from his father's house. He struggled to stay awake during the morning services and had to endure the ireful glare of Brother Bernard on more than one occasion. Brother Martin suggested that he should go to the infirmary – which Thomas did, but only to see how Nicholas was getting on.

Nicholas was sitting up in bed and looking much improved. The shivering had stopped, he told Thomas, and the fever was gone. Brother Silvius had said that if the healing continued to progress, then he could leave the infirmary later that day. Thomas wanted to tell him all about his trip home and what he had learned, but it wasn't really possible. Thomas needed to speak to his friend in privacy, and the infirmary was so busy there was no possibility of that. He would just have to wait until later.

In the meantime, thoughts conversed inside his head in chattering confusion. Fortunately the task he was employed in did not require too much concentration. He spent the morning making parchment, scraping treated and stretched sheepskin to remove any traces of flesh and fat, before painting it with a thick coat of paste to create a smooth writing surface. He was glad that the initial processes had already been completed – soaking the skin in stale urine and squeezing it out to remove the hairs – for they turned his stomach. As his hands worked, his brain churned revelations and inferences: Dr Langfell was an escaped convict and a fraud; Brother Alban might well have been involved in the poisoning of the Yorkist Richard Lovell; if he was, then he might well have poisoned Abbot Eidric too; Matthew Cundulus had connections with both Langfell and Alban and both had reason to want him dead; either could have been the person spotted by the doctor on the day he visited the abbey; Thomas's father was not implicated in the schemes of Brother Alban and the abbot to gain money and power. Amongst all the tumult, this latter realization was the one that brought him a little peace. It had been so uplifting to see his parents again. He had missed his mother, in particular, so much these last months. He heard again her final words as he walked out into the darkness: 'Take care, my darling. May God be with you and keep you safe.' He didn't feel safe. He felt very vulnerable, burdened with too much knowledge, for he was certain now that either Dr Langfell or Brother Alban was a murderer – and perhaps both. Such knowledge was a terrible thing to have. But what was he to do with it?

The thoughts continued to writhe in his head as he sat in the refectory at dinner, dabbing at his pottage with his bread while Brother Dominic read a passage from Revelation. Yesterday Thomas had been sure that Langfell was Matthew Cundulus's murderer, but now he was equally adamant that it was the prior. The link with Richard Lovell and the poisoning was too much of a coincidence. Matthew Cundulus had recognized Brother Alban just after discovering the Death's Angel mushrooms, and surely that was why he had said 'interesting' – because he had made the poison link too. Brother Alban had realized he had been spotted and had murdered Matthew Cundulus. But why had he cut out the doctor's heart and tongue? As a sign that he had stopped him from talking? Because he saw a use for the parts? Did the heart that was now in the reliquary in the abbey church belong to Matthew Cundulus and not St Augustine?

Thomas recalled the conversation that he had overheard in the reredorter between Brother Symeon and Brother Alban, and the latter's chilling statement that Father Eidric could not stand in their way and nor could anyone else. He had sounded like a man who would stop at nothing – not even murder – to get his way. Thomas looked around the refectory. Father Gregory was in his place, but Brother Alban was absent – and so too was Brother Luke. This wasn't uncommon – the librarian was probably poring over some manuscript, completely oblivious to the time. He was, as he had often said, far more interested in feeding the mind than the stomach. Thomas would take some food to the library for him, as he had several times before. While he was in the library he would be safe too, although it would only be a matter of time before Alban found him and asked him about his meeting with his father. Then what would he say? Would his face betray what he knew?

However, as it happened, this confrontation was never to take place, for late that afternoon Brother Alban fell violently ill. The first Thomas learned of it was when he saw Nicholas after Vespers, following his release from the infirmary.

'The prior is sick,' he said sombrely. 'Brother Silvius is treating him.'

'What ails him?' Thomas asked.

'His is vomiting terribly,' Nicholas answered. 'Brother Silvius fears he has the same complaint as Father Eidric.'

Thomas frowned. 'He can't have,' he murmured. 'Abbot Eidric was poisoned with Death's Angel mushrooms and it was Brother Alban who was responsible. I am sure of it.'

Nicholas returned his friend's perplexed gaze with a troubled look of his own. 'Then,' he concluded, 'Brother Alban has poisoned himself too.'

'Liam,' the voice calls, over and again. The voice is familiar yet odd. It is not how I am used to hearing it. 'Liam.' Soft, pleading, desperate. The sound echoes around me as if I'm at the bottom of a well that I can't climb out of. The walls are too high and the light above it too bright. I'm not ready. 'Let me be,' I whisper soundlessly. A hand reaches out and touches my head, fingers kneading, caressing. I can feel them through the flesh down to the bone. I can feel them, drawing me up and out. 'Not yet,' I insist silently. 'Not yet.'

CHAPTER 30

Thomas woke sweating in the rancid gloom. For an instant he smelled what his father had smelled the previous night – the stench of unwashed flesh, fetid breath. It repulsed him. He got up, took a clean tunic from the chest in the dormitory and went down the day stairs to the cloisters. Stripping off his habit and tunic, he stood naked in the moonlight and washed himself from head to foot with the cold water in the lavatorium. It made him gasp and shiver. He shook the water off his skin like a dog, then dried himself with his habit, before putting on the clean tunic. Never in his life, he reflected, had washing felt so good.

He had slept so little these past couple of nights that by rights he should have been dead on his feet, but he wasn't. His mind was wide awake. At chapter that morning Father Gregory spoke gravely of Brother Alban and led the order in prayers for the stricken prior. Brother Silvius confirmed that the symptoms were identical to the late abbot's. As most of the monks were of the belief that Abbot Eidric had died from the sweating sickness, they were naturally worried that this latest outbreak might claim more victims. Thomas, of course, knew better. He knew that Brother Alban had been poisoned. He just didn't know by who. One thing he felt sure of – it wasn't self-inflicted, as Nicholas had suggested. That just didn't fit with the man at all. Why would he kill himself? Out of guilt, contrition, desperation? None of these matched up with the Brother Alban that Thomas had been speaking with just two days before. He had been bullish, ambitious, composed, threatening – with no trace of self-doubt. No, Brother Alban had been poisoned, but not by his own hand.

It was more and more bewildering. Each time Thomas thought he knew who the murderer was, something happened to change his mind. At this rate, no one would be above suspicion. Take Brother Silvius, for example. He was a medical man; he would know about poisons. He could have poisoned Father Eidric and Brother Alban and blamed, as indeed he had, some other cause for their condition, like the sweating sickness. Then he would have had to kill Matthew Cundulus to stop him revealing the truth. He had certainly seemed keen not to enquire too deeply into the abbot's death. 'A mind can be too inquisitive,' he had warned Thomas. 'Sometimes it is better to go for the easy answer.' But why should he have wanted to kill Abbot Eidric? He was devoted to him. Besides, Thomas liked Brother Silvius. The infirmarian was dedicated to healing; he was no killer. And yet . . . Thomas needed to have a proper talk with Nicholas, to see if he had any ideas. He went to find him in the library, but Brother Luke said he had been summoned urgently to the infirmary to assist Brother Silvius in tending Brother Alban, who had taken a serious turn for the worse.

'He was in a great hurry,' Brother Luke observed, adding with a wry smile, 'but that is not an unaccustomed occurrence with young Nicholas. He has yet to learn the virtue of patience.' The librarian wagged his large head. 'I fear he will never make a copyist.'

Thomas sat at his writing desk to do some illustration while he waited for Nicholas's return. As he worked, a solitary fly buzzed insistently about him, disturbing the peace of the library as surely as his thoughts were disturbing his peace of mind. He had come to this place expecting to find tranquillity and spiritual harmony, not death, murder, intrigue, necromancy . . . It seemed as if there were more peace and security to be found in the world beyond the abbey walls.

He looked down at Father Eidric's words, encouraging his fellow brethren to pursue the godly path of humility and sacrifice and inner truth. 'Heed ye not the senseless clamour of the world of men,' he cajoled, 'but hearken instead to the glorious singing of the angels.' Was he looking down now from on high, Thomas wondered, wringing his hands at the state of his flock?

Thomas studied the work before him with a critical eye. In his distracted state, he had, not surprisingly, made errors. He put down his quill and reached for his scraper. It was blunted and he was concerned that using it might damage the parchment. He would borrow Nicholas's. He got up and went over to Nicholas's desk. He looked at the incunabula lying there with a rueful smile. Brother Luke was right about Nicholas's copying skills. The writing was uneven and marred by untidy emendations. If the work Nicholas had been undertaking had been a sacred text, it would never have passed the librarian's strict censorship, but he was a great deal more indulgent when it came to incunabulae, which he considered to be of minor importance.

Thomas picked up his friend's scraper and scrutinized it. Perhaps because Nicholas had to make such frequent use of the scraper, he usually made sure that the point was kept fine and sharp. But today the point was smudged with wax. Thomas's gaze shifted to the small wax tablet that Nicholas used for making notes – and saw a message scratched there. He frowned as he realized it was addressed to him: *Thomas. Meet me novice room. Danger. Brother l.* The message looked as if it had been composed in haste and ended abruptly, presumably when Nicholas had been called away. *Danger*, Thomas read again. *Brother l.* His mind started churning again, trying to make sense of what his friend had written. Brother l. Brother Luke? Something nagged at Thomas. He looked up at the bookshelves. The library was the heart of knowledge in the monastery. Brother Luke knew these books intimately, as his friends. Dorian's tome, for example. Brother Luke knew its contents thoroughly. And there was something else. Very recent. Empty places at table. Brother Luke and Brother Alban. A cold tingle ran down Thomas's spine.

'So you have seen it too.' Thomas jerked at the sound of the librarian's voice as if it were a string pulling at him. 'It's a pity, but, alas, I shall have to take action.' Thomas froze for an instant. But as he heard the librarian's halting step crossing the room towards him, he turned and fled.

Mum and I are walking in a garden together. I am young and it is a hot summer's day. The garden is in the grounds of an old abbey and is beautiful. In the bright sunshine, the colours are brilliantly intense. We walk through patches of light and shade, holding hands. I like the garden but I am enjoying the feel of Mum's hand in mine much more. She is wearing a red check dress and she is smiling. I love it when she smiles – especially on a lovely sunny day like this. I am very happy. We walk into a small walled bit of the garden that is full of white roses. We stand in the middle and they surround us in all their frilly, fragrant, full-bloom glory. One of the roses has fallen off its bush and lies on the sun-splashed grass. Mum walks over and picks it up and takes a deep sniff. 'Ah,' she says. 'Heavenly.'

I copy her and sniff it too. 'Heavenly,' I mimic her and she laughs.

'I'm going to tell you something, Liam,' she says, still smiling. 'It's a secret.'

I look at her, not sure whether to smile or frown. I'm not sure I want to know the secret. But she leans down and she cups her hand over my ear and she whispers her secret. Then the rose drops and spills its petals and a car crashes into a concrete wall.

I know. Finally, I know.

CHAPTER 31

He went first to the novices' room, but there was no sign of Nicholas. He did not tarry. He went back out through the cloisters to the church, entering the door into the south transept. Sunlight blazed in glory through the perpendicular window above the almost completed high altar. The presbytery was a juxtaposition of the secular and the sacred, in the form of temporarily abandoned ladders, buckets and workmen's tools and the jewelled reliquary containing the abbey's holy relics – the leg bone of St Anselm, the hand of St Geronimus, the heart of St Augustine . . .

The church was filled with a profound and surprising silence. It was the first time in months that Thomas had been in the church alone, without the presence of monks, pilgrims or workmen. The peace was so intense that he closed his eyes for a moment, overwhelmed by the sense of God all about him in the walls, ceiling, floor, windows, in every stone and timber, in the dusty air. But there was a sense of danger too, outside, approaching. At any moment he might hear a lame step at the cloister door.

It was another sound, however, that broke the silence: the clink of metal. It had come from the south transept, but was too light to be the latch of the door. Thomas turned, anxiety changing to relief as he realized the source of the sound: the sacristy. Brother Martin, of course! In his new role as sacristan, he was preparing the vessels for Mass. Thomas hurried across the transept and pushed open the small door to the sacristy. Brother Martin was crouching down, putting a vessel away in the cupboard.

'Father!' Thomas said urgently.

The novice master looked round in surprise. 'Thomas?' he said questioningly, rising up. 'What is it, my son?'

Thomas glanced back at the open door. 'I – I think I know who killed Abbot Eidric,' he stammered.

Brother Martin's reaction was totally unexpected. He smiled, laughed briefly, though there was no humour in his eyes. 'I *know* who killed Father Eidric,' he said simply.

'You do?'

'Yes. I knew when you told me of the conversation between Brother Alban and Brother Symeon in the reredorter. It all became clear.'

Thomas frowned. 'You think *they* killed the abbot?'

Brother Martin nodded. 'Brother Alban with his greed and Brother Symeon with his lust for ecclesiastical glory. Father Eidric stood in both their paths. Did you not hear them say as much?'

'Yes,' Thomas agreed hesitantly, 'but—'

'And now God in his wrath has brought them both to judgement.' Brother Martin looked quizzically at Thomas. 'Was that not what you were going to tell me?'

'No, Father,' Thomas said.

'You think someone else was responsible for the abbot's death?'

Thomas nodded.

Brother Martin's gaze softened, his eyes full of solace. 'You seem troubled, Thomas. Sit. Tell me what you know.'

Thomas sat down on a wooden stool and Brother Martin sat opposite him, a small table between them, on top of which was the heavy black glass smoothing stone and the sacristan's white alb. He felt more at ease now that Brother Martin had locked the sacristy door. 'There is so much to tell,' Thomas began, 'so much confusion. I have heard and seen so many things.'

'Take your time, my son,' the novice master cajoled. He gestured towards the locked door. 'We shall not be disturbed. Tell me all.'

Thomas took a deep breath. He thought back to when this had all started – to the day, many months ago, when Father Eidric had fallen ill at Vespers. So much had happened since then. He recalled Matthew Cundulus's visit and what he had said about the abbot's condition not being due to natural causes, his discovery of the mushrooms and recognition of someone in the abbey that Thomas had first taken for the necromancer Dr Langfell, but subsequently believed to be Brother Alban. He recalled too the doctor's warning that these were dangerous times and how prophetic his words had turned out to be when he himself had been so savagely murdered. The sequence of events and discoveries unravelled in his mind: finding out about the effect of the Death's Angel mushrooms in the writings of Brother Dorian; the conversation that Nicholas had overheard between Brother Alban and Father Gregory; the events of the night when he and Nicholas had observed Dr Langfell practising his black arts. All this was known to Brother Martin. But he didn't know of more recent events and listened with keen attention as Thomas spoke of his meeting with Brother Alban in the warming room and his subsequent trip home. His interest deepened as Thomas related his conversation with his father and what he had learned about Dr Langfell and the poisoning of Richard Lovell and the part

Brother Alban, it seemed, had played in it.

'So I am right,' Brother Martin remarked, 'Brother Alban is a poisoner. I knew there was something dark in his past when he came here, but I did not know it was murder. Not that it would have mattered to Father Eidric. He was a man of such forgiveness and mercy that as long as he believed a sinner to be truly repentant, he would happily offer him a second chance, just as he did with Ambrose.' His lips lifted in an expression of disgust. 'See how they have repaid his kindness. He was betrayed by them as surely as Our Lord was betrayed by Judas Iscariot. Like him, they will surely be damned to eternity.'

The uncharacteristic vehemence of this outburst seemed to drain Brother Martin. He looked down at the table, his fingers touching the smoothing stone distractedly.

It was Thomas who broke the silence. 'I know that Brother Alban may have had good reason to kill Father Eidric and also Matthew Cundulus,' he said haltingly, 'but I do not understand why he would poison himself, just as his plans were succeeding. It does not make sense.'

'Things do not always make sense, Thomas,' Brother Martin responded quietly. 'Compunction may make its home even in as black a heart as Alban's.' He looked up, his vivid blue eyes staring deep into Thomas's. 'But you have not told me who you believe to be responsible.'

Thomas hesitated. Then: 'Brother Luke,' he said.

'Brother Luke!'

'Yes. He is a man of great knowledge. He knows Brother Dorian's book. I am sure he knows of the mushrooms and their deadly effect. Yesterday he was absent from dinner and so was Brother Alban. It was after that that the prior fell ill. And today I found a note from Nicholas scratched in the wax tablet on his writing desk.' He told Brother Martin about the message he had found. 'The last word was unfinished but I am sure it was "Luke" he was going to write. He was warning me of Brother Luke.' He shivered as he heard again Brother Luke's voice saying, 'I shall have to take action,' and his shuffling step on the library floor.

Brother Martin shook his head incredulously. 'What possible reason would Brother Luke have for murdering Father Eidric, whom he loved and respected above all men in the world? He would have laid down his life for his abbot, just as I would have also.'

Thomas stared at the novice master in confusion. There was nothing, he realized suddenly, he could reply. It was true – he had not thought about the librarian's motive, not *why* but only *how*. Had he formed too hasty a judgement – something he had been guilty of a number of times these past days? He had bumbled from one accusation to another as new facts were uncovered. Now that he considered the facts in the light of Brother Martin's objection, he saw there was no real evidence against Brother Luke. Just vague – very vague – suspicions. Not for the first time these past days, he suddenly felt out of his depth, immersed in affairs that were beyond the range of his age and experience.

'Brother Alban murdered Father Eidric,' Brother Martin declared, 'in collusion with Brother Symeon, because Father Eidric would have nothing to do with their schemes for money and influence.' He gestured in dismissive disapproval at a pile of incunabulae beside him. 'You cannot buy your way into Heaven. These indulgences are not worth the paper they are printed on.' He picked one up, crumpled it in his hand. 'I shall burn them all.'

'But Father Gregory is still abbot. He may not agree.'

'Father Gregory will have the bishop to answer to shortly, and Bishop Ivan is not a man to take heresy lightly. Necromancy is a black art and punishable by excommunication.'

'Then we shall need a new abbot.'

'If that is what the bishop decides.'

'And what of Doctor Langfell?'

'That charlatan! He has left already – and taken his cur, Ambrose, with him.'

Thomas looked at the novice master. Perhaps there might yet be a good end to all these terrible events, he reflected, for surely it would be a happy outcome were Brother Martin to become abbot. The monastery needed true, devout leadership after these dark days. Thomas thought again about Brother Alban. Was it possible after all that he had taken the mushrooms himself in a sudden fit of repentance? No, he could not believe that. But with the bishop's arrival imminent, perhaps he had realized that his crimes would be uncovered and that this time he would not escape retribution. It was possible, Thomas supposed, that the awful certainty of the grisly fate that awaited him could have driven Alban to take his own life . . .

He stood and bowed slightly. He needed to return to the library and make his apologies to Brother Luke. 'Thank you for listening to me, Father,' he said humbly. 'I shall not keep you longer from your tasks.'

Brother Martin smiled. 'I should thank *you*, Thomas – we all should, for it is you who have done most to discover the truth of Father Eidric's murder. You are indeed a great asset to this monastery.'

Thomas blushed. 'I have much to learn,' he said.

'We all have much to learn, Thomas.' The novice master's eyes had regained their customary sparkle.

Thomas turned to go. As he did so, his habit swirled

and caught a vessel on the shelf of the open cupboard. It clanged onto the flagstone floor. Instinctively Thomas turned back and bent down to pick up the vessel. But his hand halted in mid air as he caught sight of what was spilled there. He had no doubt as to what it was, but stared as if hoping he might be mistaken. He'd seen them under a tree and in the illustrations of a book, and now he was looking at them spilling out of an overturned vessel on the sacristy floor: a small scattering of white and deadly Death's Angel mushrooms.

He looked up slowly, with a perplexed expression. '*You*,' he uttered incredulously. 'It was *you*.'

Part Three

CHAPTER 32

My eyes grog open on a world that is shockingly different at first, then oddly familiar. Dad's anxious face gazes down, causing new astonishment. Thoughts thrash wildly in my mind like landed fish. I shut my eyes, try to focus.

'Liam, Liam!' The voice strange, yet so familiar, breathless with amazement and excitement. I open my eyes again slowly. The face is no longer anxious but animated, exuberant. 'Liam!' Dad leans forward, hugs me, his stubble rough as glass paper on my cheek. 'I thought I'd lost you. Thank goodness you're back.' I feel dampness on my cheek and realize with yet more surprise that Dad is crying.

'It's OK,' I murmur. 'I'm OK, Dad. Really.'

I've been out for days, I discover later, in a kind of coma. The doctors did various tests but could find no cause for my condition. There seemed no apparent reason why I had lost consciousness or why I have regained it suddenly now. This puzzling element pleases Uncle Jack no end. It supports his belief in the inadequacy of science.

'Life's a mystery,' he pronounces to me that first day with the aplomb of one who has made some startling discovery. But he's right, I reflect: life *is* a mystery.

I have to stay in hospital for another couple of days – just for observation and so that the doctors can carry out a few more tests. On my second day, Father Christopher comes to visit. He brings me a present, which I'm pleased to say isn't grapes but chocolate. I open it right away and start munching. Since I've come out of 'the coma' I've been starving, and the hospital food hasn't exactly satisfied my appetite.

'It's good to see you back with us, Liam,' Father Christopher says, sitting down on a chair by my bed. 'We were all very concerned.' He asks if the doctors have found out yet what caused my condition and I tell him about the tests.

'They're baffled,' I say.

'Well, you're back, that's the important thing.' A half-moon smile rises on his round face. 'I suppose we could call it a minor miracle.'

I give a half-laugh. 'I suppose,' I concede. 'God moves in mysterious ways . . .'

I tell him a little of what I've experienced – the slip into Thomas's world – testing the waters really, watching his reaction to see if he thinks I'm totally mad, because I know I'll have to tell Dad sometime soon and that's not going to be easy. Father Christopher listens carefully, nodding now and then. I'm relieved that not once does he burst out laughing or frown at me like I've lost my marbles.

'It sounds as if the boy's spirit entered you,' he remarks when I've finished.

'Like a possession?' I wonder.

'In a way,' he says. 'But by a good spirit, not a bad one. Not one that meant you harm.'

'Have you seen spirits like that?' I ask.

Father Christopher nods. 'I've been called to perform exorcisms a few times. But I've never known anyone be possessed by a good spirit before.'

I consider this for a moment or two. 'It's almost like necromancy in reverse, isn't it?' I suggest. 'Like the spirit summoned me – and to reveal the past, not the future.'

'It seems that way,' Father Christopher agrees. He gives me one of his penetrating stares. 'Often there's a reason for these things, Liam. The possession is as much to do with the one possessed as the possessor.'

I say nothing, but I know what he means. He's talking about Mum, about what happened, about my grief. And of course he's right: my possession, coma, whatever you want to call it, told me as much about my life as about Thomas's.

Father Christopher asks me if I've told Dad what I've just told him and I shake my head.

'I will though,' I add without enthusiasm. It's not exactly something I'm looking forward to.

'Are you worried about it?' Father Christopher prompts.

'Yeah.' I nod. 'Dad's not – well, he's not into that supernatural stuff.'

Father Christopher smiles at this. 'What, religion, you mean?' he says.

'Yeah,' I reply, smiling back. 'He likes things you can see and touch, like bones.'

'I spoke to your dad a couple of times while you were away from us. He was very very worried.' He pauses an instant, then says, 'Events like this change people, Liam. Tell the truth and he'll listen.' It sounds so simple put like that, but I know it won't be.

'I'll say a prayer for you – and for your dad too,' Father Christopher says as he gets up to leave. 'I can't promise it'll have any effect, but . . .' He shrugs.

I recall our first proper meeting, when he talked of the power of prayer, and think I could certainly do with some of that now.

* * *

The next day, back home, I go to Dad's workshop. The reconstruction of the face over the skull is almost finished now. Dad's done a good job, but he hasn't got it completely right. The face bears some resemblance to Thomas but it isn't him. How could it be? Humans are made of flesh, not clay. How could you know from a skull of the freckles that speckled a forehead or the small, pale island-shaped birthmark that mapped one cheek, or the slightly lopsided smile? I study the skull, stare into its sightless eyes. I feel none of the terror or apprehension or unease I'd experienced before. I'm sad: sad at the loss, the waste, the betrayal – but these things make me angry too. And it's not only Thomas I'm angry for. At least, though, I think as I stare at his skull, his truth can be revealed: 'Brother Boniface' will no longer be just an archaeological exhibit, but the last remains of a once living, flesh-and-bones novice monk, whose story can be told. After five hundred years Thomas can finally rest in peace.

That evening I tell Dad the story. I don't know how he'll react, but I have to tell him, and I don't know if Father Christopher's prayer has worked or if just talking to him the day before has helped, but I feel more confident now. Besides, too much has been left unsaid between us this past year. First, though, I try to explain what has happened to me, how I know the story – and that's more difficult than telling the story itself. I'm still confused about it all. It seemed as if I was really there, inside Thomas's head, seeing everything he saw, thinking everything he thought, feeling everything he felt, even dreaming everything he dreamed. Like I was him – and yet I was me too.

'It's like I was living two lives at the same time,' I say. 'Like . . .' I struggle to find an image to illustrate what I mean. 'Like . . .' I'm half expecting Dad to cut me short with a dismissive remark, but he doesn't. He nods and frowns.

'Back in the dark days,' he says, 'before CDs, we used to record onto cassette tapes. Sometimes, when you taped over an old recording on a cassette that was faulty or worn, you could hear that recording underneath the new one, both recordings playing at the same time. Is that the kind of thing you mean?'

'Yes,' I reply thankfully. 'That's exactly it.'

Dad's not quite satisfied though. He offers a more scholarly example: 'In medieval times, when your monk was alive, they wrote on parchment, which wasn't the easiest thing to make – or the cheapest.' I nod – parchment-making is just one of the many things Thomas's story has taught me. 'So they quite often scratched off the writing and reused the parchment to write something new. But there was always a slight imprint left behind from the earlier writing. We call these documents palimpsests. That incunabula Wagstaff's team found was one.'

'So I'm a palimpsest,' I say with a wry grin. 'Well, it sounds better than a faulty cassette, I suppose.' But actually I prefer the cassette image. It seems to sum up my experience better.

After this exchange, things are easier. I tell the story right the way through – well, all that I remember of it, because it has faded a little now, like a dream, a very vivid dream. Dad listens quietly, even nodding encouragingly when I falter.

'So he was betrayed by the one he most trusted,' he comments when, finally, I've finished my tale. 'The one he thought of as his father.' He gazes at me with sombre, sorrowful eyes. 'I know you think I've let you down, Liam – and Mum too,' he says. 'You think I don't really care.' I shake my head, open my mouth to protest, but Dad stops me. 'You think I don't care enough.'

I take a deep breath. I've been waiting for this moment for a long time. But now things are different, so different. 'You seemed so cool,' I say. 'It was like you weren't affected. You just carried on with your work as if nothing had happened. I guess I thought it was, well, heartless.' I'm evading the truth and I know it and I can't do it any more.

Dad nods, but before he can speak, I say, 'I didn't understand why you were like you were, Dad.' My voice drops to a hoarse whisper. 'But I do now.' Dad's face takes on an expression of wary bewilderment. 'Mum's car crash,' I blurt, then swallow before continuing, 'It wasn't an accident, was it, Dad?'

Dad shakes his head and makes an exclamation of denial, but gets no further. He shuts his eyes a moment, then opens them again. It's obvious that he's finding facing the truth as hard as I am. It's so much easier to tell a white lie. But this time he doesn't. He looks me in the eye and says, 'No. No, Liam, it wasn't an accident.'

I can't leave it at that. 'Mum crashed the car deliberately, didn't she?' I persist. 'She meant to kill herself.'

Dad nods. He gets up and walks over to his bureau, where he keeps all his important stuff like passports and things. He opens a drawer and roots around among some papers. I watch him, intrigued and apprehensive. I have no idea what he's looking for but I'm certain it's not a winning lottery ticket. He takes something out of the drawer, then walks back and hands it to me. It's a piece of lined paper torn from a notebook and folded.

'What's this?' I ask, stalling.

'Open it,' Dad says.

Slowly I unfold the paper and read what's written there – a few words scrawled in Mum's hand: *I can't take any more. Sorry.*

I stare at the words till they become a liquid blur.

'I didn't show it to anyone,' Dad says. 'I didn't want anyone to know – especially not you. I wanted to protect you.'

I nod. 'I know,' I murmur. 'But you should have told me, Dad.'

'I was going to,' he says, 'but only when I thought you could cope with knowing.' He puts his hand tentatively on my shoulder. 'I loved Mum, Liam – just as I love you. When she died, it was almost like I died too. I didn't know how to express my grief – or my anger. I had a lot of anger. I couldn't even mourn properly because of it. You remember the day after Mum died, when those white roses arrived, the ones I ordered for our anniversary?'

I nod.

'Well, it was like she had thrown my love back in my face. I felt so rejected, so angry.' He sighs. 'Work was my way of coping. And when I modelled those skulls, gave them faces, it was like I was giving them back life, denying death.' He sits down on the sofa next to me and puts his arms around me. I can't believe that I got everything so wrong; that all this time I've been angry with Dad and it was Mum I should have been mad at. 'It was so terrible when I thought I'd lost you, Liam,' Dad mutters, and once again I feel his tears on my cheek, and I know these tears are not only for me, but for Mum too – at last Dad is expressing his grief. And in a moment my own eyes have welled up and I hug Dad as the tears come.

The next day I tell Uncle Jack my story, but in a shortened version – partly because I find reliving the events exhausting but also because I know the limits of my uncle's attention span. It's shorter than ever today because he's sorting his stuff out for his next trip – he's going back to Indonesia at the end of the week to be part of some rafting venture, which he says is going to make him a fortune. Predictably, he shows particular interest in the necromantic elements of Thomas's tale and asks me lots of questions about Dr Langfell's experiments.

'So he believed he could divine the future,' he muses.

'I'm not sure he believed in anything. He just told people what they wanted to hear.'

'Cynic.'

'It was just a scam, like those incunabulae. I reckon they got it about right when they called them "medieval scratch-cards". That's all they were really: just a way of taking gullible people's money.' I smile teasingly. 'Like the lottery.'

Uncle Jack rises to the bait. 'You can scoff,' he says, 'but as it happens I won last weekend.'

'Really? How much?'

Uncle Jack looks a little sheepish. 'Twenty quid,' he says, and I laugh. 'OK, it's not much but I'm on the winning track.'

'Winning track.' I shake my head disbelievingly. 'You don't really believe that, Uncle Jack, do you?'

'Certainly I do. I've just got to stick with it.'

Things haven't changed so much in five hundred years, I reflect.

I want to go back to Maundle Abbey. I'm a little worried about how it might affect me, but I feel it's something I need to do to put this whole business to rest. Dad has deep misgivings, but eventually he agrees to take me. I think he realizes that he can't just treat me like a child any more. Too much has happened. I feel like I've grown up by years in the last week or so.

'It'd probably be quite a good thing for me to go anyway,' he concedes. 'There are a few things I need to talk to Wagstaff and his team about.' He pulls a face. 'No doubt he'll want to see the finished skull and invent some more wild theories.'

We drive down to the abbey that afternoon. It's a gloomy, overcast day, the sky a shabby quilt of grey and off-white. The ruined monastery looks grim and desolate. Dad goes to find Wagstaff, while, as before, I enter the monastery. I'm carrying a bunch of white roses that I bought from a roadside seller near the gate. It was an impulse purchase – I don't even know what I'm going to do with them. Somehow it seems fitting, though, that I should be walking into the abbey carrying Mum's favourite kind of flower and the Yorkist symbol – the white rose of the house of York.

I wander from room to ruined room, the geography of Thomas's story: the refectory where he and the other monks sat in silence and ate to the accompaniment of readings from the Bible; the novices' room, with its magnificent vaulted ceiling, where Thomas and Nicholas spent so much time together; the warming room, with its double fireplace, where the ink was stored and Thomas encountered Brother Alban . . . I stand in the cloisters by the stone lavatorium where Thomas washed himself in the moonlight after his trip home. Then I enter the chapter house and sit on what is left of the benches, looking down at the remains of the graves of former abbots – one of which, I suppose, is Eidric's. A slideshow of vivid images passes through my mind: Ambrose's cruel chastisement, Dr Langfell's introduction and the incident of the onychomancy. It's like I'm seeing slides of my own life.

I still don't understand what happened to me. Did I by some weird psychic phenomenon go back five hundred years and share the mind and body of a novice monk called Thomas? Or, in my emotionally traumatized state (as the therapists would no doubt have it), did I just imagine it all? I asked Dad this question last night. I expected him to go for the imagining theory – he is a scientist, after all – but again he surprised me. 'I don't know, Liam,' he said with a humility that I don't think I've ever seen in him before. 'But one thing's for sure – if it is all imagination, then you have a great career ahead of you as an author.'

Out in the cloisters once more, I stand for a moment, shutting my eyes, listening. I can hear the deep hum of the wind, the twittering of birds, the noise of men at work in the church – a soundscape similar surely to the one Thomas would have known. These were the sounds that would have accompanied his last hurried passage through these cloisters over five hundred years ago – though, of course, he had not known his end would come so soon.

I enter the church through the south door, just as Thomas did that day, but I go straight to the sacristy. I'm a little apprehensive when I pass through the archway, because this is where I fell into my 'coma' and I've no wish to repeat that experience. But it's different this time: I know the ending. I've already lived it.

I look around. There's no table, no wooden stools, no cupboard, no vessels or vestments or smoothing stone; the room is totally empty, yet I see it in my head exactly as it was that fateful day. But I'm detached now, no longer a participant, but a witness. I see the look of incredulity on Thomas's face as he gazes up at his mentor and I share his anguish as he struggles to come to terms with the realization that Brother Martin, the man he trusted and revered above all others, is a murderer.

CHAPTER 33

'It was God's command, Thomas. *"Vengeance is mine," saith the Lord.* I was but his instrument.' Brother Martin spoke in a tone of quiet reason that was in marked contrast to the anguish of Thomas's accusation.

'You poisoned Brother Alban, and Father Eidric—'

'No!' Brother Martin raised one palm. 'No, I would never have harmed Abbot Eidric. He was a father to me. Brother Alban murdered him, just as I told you, with the collusion of Brother Symeon.'

'And you have killed Brother Alban.'

'The Lord commanded me. His wickedness was manifold and obscene. He would have destroyed this house, besmirched its reputation, brought hatred and ignominy upon us. I had to stop him.'

'You murdered him!'

'His soul is already in Hell for what he has done.'

Thomas gazed at the novice master with an expression of pained bewilderment. 'And Matthew Cundulus? What of him?'

'I believe you may lay that crime at Ambrose's door.'

'Ambrose!'

'Yes, Ambrose. You observed, I think, from his heinous carving how skilfully he wielded a knife.'

'But murder?'

'He had little choice, poor fool. Matthew Cundulus had recognized Langfell, and possibly Brother Alban too. They were together at the time on their way to see Father Gregory. Each had too much to lose by being discovered, so they "persuaded" Ambrose to dispense with the physician, no doubt threatening him with terrible chastisement should he fail to do so. He would have done anything to avoid that. They also ordered him to remove the heart and tongue for their nefarious purposes.'

Thomas considered this shocking revelation in silence for an instant or two. Then, 'How do you know this?' he asked.

'I went to see Doctor Langfell,' Brother Martin explained, 'following our conversation after chapter, the day he demonstrated his black arts. I said I would see him hang if he did not tell me all. It was not difficult to get him to confess. The man seemed to revel in the darkness of his deeds.'

'And you let him go?'

'He is nothing to me. Let him take his evil practices elsewhere. The hangman will catch up with him eventually.'

Without the good humour that usually characterized his eyes, Brother Martin cut a sinister figure. He continued to speak with utter calm, as if nothing they had talked about was of any great consequence. To Thomas, however, these revelations were so momentous it was as if the abbey's foundations were crumbling beneath them. He was certain too that there were more to come. He recalled his earlier unease at the circumstances of the sacristan's death.

'Brother Symeon's fall was no accident, was it?' he prompted. 'You pushed him.'

'No,' Brother Martin refuted. 'I would have had I been able to persuade the sanctimonious coward to climb the ladder, but he was much too frightened. The very prospect set him jibbering. In the end I found a more fitting means to deal with him.' His eyes lowered to the smoothing stone on the table in front of him.

'You used that?' Thomas queried.

'It made an excellent weapon. Two blows and he was gurgling his last. All I had to do was arrange his body and the ladder to make it look like he'd fallen.' Again the novice master's tone belied the violence of the deeds he was describing. 'You were the only one, Thomas, to express doubt – which is much to your credit. Your intelligence and intellectual curiosity are greatly to be admired.'

'I don't want such admiration,' Thomas muttered with weary bitterness. He was appalled suddenly at the inappropriateness of Brother Martin's remark – his whole tone throughout their exchange in fact. They were talking about murder – four murders (although Brother Alban was not dead yet, he very soon would be), two of which had been committed by Brother Martin himself, the man who was supposed to be his spiritual father and guide, his example. Abbot Eidric would surely be looking down and weeping.

Thomas thought again of Brother Luke. He felt a pang of shame at having considered that he might be a murderer. He had behaved inexcusably to the librarian, who had shown him nothing but kindness, encouragement and guidance. Recalling the scene in the library, a new worry arose in him. He knew now that the name Nicholas had not finished writing on his wax tablet was not 'Luke' but 'Martin' and, having revealed the note's contents to the novice master, he was sure that Brother Martin knew too. Unwittingly, Thomas had put his friend in mortal danger. But it was too late to change that now.

'Nicholas knows,' he said.

'So I had surmised. I imagine he must have heard Brother Alban say something in his fever.'

'What will you do?'

'I shall talk with Nicholas, as I have talked with you. The ravings of a sick man can easily be discounted.' Brother Martin gave Thomas an uncompromising stare. 'Nicholas will be no trouble. He will do as you do.'

'And what will I do?'

'What is best for this monastery: say nothing.'

His words reminded Thomas of something similar that Brother Alban had said to him when they'd talked in the warming room. Everyone, it seemed, had the best interests of the monastery at heart – or claimed that they had. He took a deep breath. 'And then what will happen?' he enquired.

'Brother Alban will die and Father Eidric will have been avenged,' Brother Martin stated matter-of-factly. 'The bishop will come and Father Gregory will be disgraced. There will be a new abbot and, the Lord be willing, this house shall return to the path of righteousness and sanctity, and accomplish the godly and charitable works for which it was ordained.'

'But how can that be?' Thomas exclaimed. 'No good can come from murder.'

'Not murder, Thomas, justice, revenge.'

Thomas tossed his head in outrage. 'You value vengeance above flesh and bone. Just as Father Gregory values power and Brother Alban gold. This house is rotten to the core.'

Brother Martin smiled indulgently. 'Sometimes, Thomas, the end justifies the means by which it is achieved,' he said. 'This order is greater than any of us. We must do all we can to preserve it. We are living on a knife edge as it is. The people no longer respect or revere us as they did. The worm is turning.'

Thomas threw up a hand in disgust. 'If people do not respect us, it is because we trick them with old bones and false relics, and fleece them with incunabulae, and grow rich while they starve, and commit murder without compunction,' he declared vehemently.

Brother Martin nodded appreciatively. 'You are right, Thomas, and your anger is just and admirable. We must put aside our sinful practices and return to the true way of Saint Benedict.' His light-blue eyes were indulgences offering Thomas everything. 'One day, I believe, you shall be abbot of this place.'

Thomas was not to be won over. 'I don't want to be abbot. I don't even want to be a monk any more. I want to go home.'

'*This* is your home,' said Brother Martin simply. 'You have given your life into the service of God.'

'I cannot serve God in this place because he isn't here,' Thomas riposted. 'This is the Devil's house.'

'You cannot leave, Thomas.'

But Thomas had made up his mind. 'No one can stop me. I know too much.'

'That is precisely why you cannot leave. You know too much, and knowledge is a dangerous, dangerous thing.'

Thomas's anger turned to contempt. 'You are scared I will denounce you.'

'I do not think of myself,' Brother Martin said wearily. 'I think only of this house and its future. Nothing can be allowed to endanger that.'

'How can you say that when it is you who has done more than any man to endanger it?' Thomas retorted. Brother Martin, he thought, was like the ink that was so acidic it destroyed the parchment it wrote upon. He tightened the cincture around his waist in a gesture of finality and turned to leave.

'Thomas, I cannot allow you to go.'

Thomas faced the novice master again with unwavering resolve, but in which there was a hint of sadness, for this was the man he had trusted above all others. 'You have no authority over me now,' he said. 'There is nothing you can do to stop me.'

'But I must, Thomas.' Brother Martin's hand touched upon the smoothing stone. Once again Thomas turned to leave. Brother Martin picked up the smoothing stone in both hands.

'Thomas!' he called, already moving. 'Don't do this.'

But Thomas carried on walking towards the door. He reached out to turn the key in the lock, but before he could do so, something rock-like bludgeoned into the back of his head – once and then again, smashing his skull. He cried out with the searing pain. Then his legs splayed under him and he fell, dropping down, down, down into brightness without end, and silence.

Chapter 34

I stand in the choir facing the altar – a magnificent stone island surrounded by deep holes and wooden planks. Sunlight beams reverently through the giant glassless perpendicular window. On a scaffolding tower to my left a man taps delicately at a plaster wall, la-la-ing melodically as he works. He is not singing loudly yet his voice seems to fill the whole presbytery. I feel a sudden frisson of euphoria. I close my eyes and, through the veil of swirling orange, Thomas appears in his habit and sandals; then he fades and a new image forms, a woman's face gazing down adoringly. It puzzles me at first, then I realize it's the image of the Virgin Mary at the Nativity from Thomas's favourite book, *The Mirror of the Blessed Life of Jesus Christ*. Gradually this picture fades too, or morphs rather into Mum. She is wearing a red check dress from when I was a child and she is smiling.

A hand settles on my shoulder. I open my eyes and see Dad standing next to me.

'You OK?' he asks. There's a new tinge of concern to his voice these days.

'Yeah, fine,' I assure him. 'It's so peaceful here.'

'It is,' he agrees.

'I closed my eyes and I saw him,' I say. 'And I saw Mum too. She was smiling.'

'That's good,' Dad says. 'I'm glad she was smiling.'

'Yeah.'

We stand in silence, listening to the workman's gentle tapping and singing. The sounds wrap around me like a cloak, a habit. The cloak seems to wrap around Dad too, binding us together. I feel somehow like Uncle Jack should be here too with me and Dad . . . and Mum – our whole small family. I say this to Dad. He smiles sort of sadly.

'Jack,' he says in a kind of sigh, with a slight shake of the head. 'Jack. He won't ever settle down.' He sighs again. 'I used to envy him, you know, Liam. That lifestyle, all that travelling, no responsibility . . . There were times when it seemed like a perfect life. But now . . . He has no home, he has no wife, he has no child, he has no vocation, no real purpose in life – and no Mum, no Laura.'

I frown. 'But he and Mum didn't get on.'

'Not on the surface, no. But he was always a little in love

with her. And, though he drove her mad, she cared for him deeply. She got angry with him because she thought he was wasting his life.' Dad looked at me. 'He could have been a doctor, Liam, but he dropped out of medical school. It was too much like hard work and, as you know, Jack doesn't like hard work. I think he regrets now that he didn't go through with it.'

'But he always seems so – so carefree, so jolly.' I am struggling to come to terms with this new portrait of Uncle Jack – this sad, unfulfilled drifter, wandering from place to place aimlessly, gambling, waiting for something to happen, lacking control, a kind of Ambrose-like figure. It's an Uncle Jack I've never seen. But then nor had I seen the true nature of his relationship with Mum. I'd always thought they couldn't stand each other. There are so many things, it seems, I haven't understood. I guess that just like Thomas five hundred years ago, I'm finding out how hard adults are to read.

'I found something I think you'll be interested in,' Dad says now, and he hands me a sheet of printed paper. 'It's from an information pack that Wagstaff's been distributing – and, for once, it actually contains some proper information.'

I study the sheet. It's headed 'Maundle Abbey, Dissolution'.

Maundle Abbey was dissolved in 1537 following the execution of its twenty-third and final abbot, Martin Haycocke, whose reign had lasted thirty-eight years. The abbot was arrested on charges of treason arising from his support for the Pilgrimage of Grace, a popular rebellion against the suppression of the monasteries and its enforcer, Henry VIII's chief minister Thomas Cromwell. Abbot Martin was tried in York on 9th April 1537 and pleaded guilty to all charges, avowing that he had done his duty before God and the Holy Mother Church. He was hanged the next day.

'So your monk's murderer got his comeuppance,' Dad comments.

'Eventually,' I say. 'He must have been ancient by the time he died.'

'Let's hope he used the time well,' says Dad; 'to make amends, I mean.'

'Nothing could make amends for what he did,' I say, but I'm not really thinking about Brother Martin. Who do you punish when someone kills themself? I wonder suddenly. But I quickly rein the thought in. 'Do you think he killed Nicholas too?' I say.

'Maybe,' Dad replies. 'It was a very different world then, Liam. Even the popes weren't above murder. Life didn't mean so much.'

A living picture enters my head of Thomas's mum running into the parlour and embracing him, the night he walked from the monastery – her face aglow with happiness and adoration. 'Thomas's mum must have been devastated when she heard he'd died,' I say.

'If she ever did. I imagine Thomas just "disappeared".'

'Well, that would have been pretty devastating, wouldn't it? If she thought he'd just run off, turned his back on God and the Church. And on her.' That's the crux of it, isn't it, I think – the awful feeling of abandonment. This gut-churning, chest-cramping feeling I'm going to wake up with every day, knowing Mum killed herself. I wonder for a moment whether it would have been better if she had just disappeared – but of course it wouldn't have been. At least this way there's a chance I might find peace one day, however distant that day might be.

I step forward over the wooden plank to the altar. I glance down at the hollowed place in which Thomas lay for so many years. I cross myself and put the bunch of white roses carefully on top of the altar, the way people put flowers on a loved one's grave. 'Goodbye,' I whisper. 'God bless you.' It's a sort of prayer, I suppose, like the one Father Christopher said that day I went to talk to him. I don't know what or if I believe; it's one of the many things I'm going to have to think hard about in the days and weeks to come, but Thomas did

– right to the end – and I say the words in respect for him. And they can't harm Mum, can they?

And in that instant I know what I'm going to do with Mum's ashes trapped in that awful tacky plastic urn. I know Dad thinks I'm too attached to them, that I treat them somehow like people back in Thomas's day treated holy relics or those sick people at Lourdes treat their holy water – as if they or it had some magical property. But I don't think that. It's just that I feel closer to Mum having her ashes around. They've given me comfort, the way those animal skulls did Thomas. But the time's come now to let go; it *is* kind of morbid to share your bedroom with your mum's ashes, I can see that – like wishing for a coffin. I'd thought about bringing the ashes with me today and scattering them here on the altar, but I'm not ready to give them up like that – and, besides, this isn't a happy place. I'm going to persuade Dad to bury them somewhere – it doesn't have to be in a churchyard or a cemetery, but somewhere with a proper headstone, so that there will be a special place where I can go and feel close to Mum. And try to understand what she did. And maybe pray too in my own way. I might even ask Father Christopher to say a few words over the burial place. Yes, I'd like that.

I stand for a moment, thinking about all this, watching motes of dust dance like angels in the sunlit air. Then I turn and walk back towards Dad.